Acclaim for the authors of
Holiday with a Vampire

MAUREEN CHILD

"Maureen Child is one of the stars in the ascendant...poised for the next big step."
—*Publishers Weekly*

"Child excellently unravels the mystery... without slowing the momentum of the love story.... It's very easy to fall in love with this heroic and sexy couple."
—*Romantic Times BOOKreviews* on *Nevermore*

CARIDAD PIÑEIRO

"Anne Rice, move over. This Cuban-American writer sucks up to the 'vampire romance' genre with a Latin vengeance..."
—*Latina Magazine* on *Darkness Calls*

"Once again the audience will believe that vampires exist.... In an incredibly short time, Caridad Piñeiro is proving to be one the sub-genre's b
—*The*

D1019627

MAUREEN CHILD

is a *USA TODAY* bestselling author of more than ninety novels, including historicals, paranormal historicals, contemporary romances and series romances. Her books have won numerous awards, including a Prism and an Award of Excellence. She's a three-time RITA® Award nominee, a finalist for a National Reader's Choice Award, and one of her books, *A Pocketful of Paradise*, was made into a CBS-TV movie called *The Soul Collector.*

Maureen lives in Southern California's OC, with her pretty cool husband, two kids and the still-entertaining ghost of her golden retriever, Abbey. Visit Maureen Child online at www.maureenchild.com.

CARIDAD PIÑEIRO

was born in Havana, Cuba, and settled in the New York metropolitan area. Caridad's novels have been nominated for various readers' and reviewers' choice awards, including the *Affaire de Coeur*, Harlequin and RIO awards. *Danger Calls* was a 2005 Top 5 Read from *Catalina* magazine and the first book selected for *Catalina's* cyber book club.

When not writing, Caridad is a mom, wife and attorney. For more information on Caridad's books, contests and appearances, or to contact Caridad, please visit www.caridad.com.

HOLIDAY WITH A VAMPIRE

MAUREEN CHILD AND CARIDAD PIÑEIRO

Silhouette Books

n⦿cturne™

If you purchased this book without a cover you should be aware
that this book is stolen property. It was reported as "unsold and
destroyed" to the publisher, and neither the author nor the
publisher has received any payment for this "stripped book."

SILHOUETTE BOOKS

ISBN-13: 978-0-373-61776-0
ISBN-10:   0-373-61776-3

HOLIDAY WITH A VAMPIRE

Copyright © 2007 by Harlequin Books S.A.

The publisher acknowledges the copyright holders
of the individual works as follows:

CHRISTMAS CRAVINGS
Copyright © 2007 by Maureen Child

FATE CALLS
Copyright © 2007 by Caridad Piñeiro Scordato

All rights reserved. Except for use in any review, the reproduction
or utilization of this work in whole or in part in any form by any
electronic, mechanical or other means, now known or hereafter
invented, including xerography, photocopying and recording, or in
any information storage or retrieval system, is forbidden without
the written permission of the editorial office, Silhouette Books,
233 Broadway, New York, NY 10279 U.S.A.

This is a work of fiction. Names, characters, places and incidents are
either the product of the author's imagination or are used fictitiously, and
any resemblance to actual persons, living or dead, business establishments,
events or locales is entirely coincidental.

This edition published by arrangement with Harlequin Books S.A.

® and TM are trademarks of Harlequin Books S.A., used under license.
Trademarks indicated with ® are registered in the United States Patent
and Trademark Office, the Canadian Trade Marks Office and in other
countries.

www.silhouettenocturne.com

Printed in U.S.A.

CONTENTS

CHRISTMAS CRAVINGS

MAUREEN CHILD

With love to my mom, Sallye Carberry,
for always reading, catching my typos
and being the best mom ever!

Chapter 1

Grayson Stone felt the dawn coming and knew he couldn't escape it.

He stirred in the snow, his body splayed in the center of a neatly tended yard, and wondered for a second where the hell he was. Then he remembered. A vague echo of a memory danced through his dazed mind. He'd come back to Whisper, Wyoming, as he had every year since his death.

It was the week before Christmas and he'd come here to hide away. To forget. To remember. To lose himself in the serene quiet of what was still a wilderness.

He blinked and focused his eyes on a nearby

bush—carefully pruned into the shape of a lopsided elephant—and told himself that the wilderness had done some changing.

But what did it matter? The pounding ache in his head, the lethargy of his body, the creeping sluggishness moving through his system incrementally told him that he didn't have enough time to think these questions through, anyway. He shifted his gaze to the lightening sky. Already, that broad, sweeping expanse was a faint shade of lavender, heralding the coming sun. And while he watched the day begin, he thought about just how long it had been since the last time he'd seen a sunrise.

One hundred and fifty years.

Times had been so different then. Hell, *he* had been different, then. Alive, for one. And not in danger of combusting in the first rays of dawn.

"Ironic or poetic that I should die here again?" he whispered, just to hear a sound other than the soft sigh of the wind through the bushes. He'd spent most of his undead life far from Wyoming and the memories that haunted this place. And yet, it seemed that Fate had a sense of humor. He'd come home to die a second time.

His skin prickled with the coming of the sun. It felt as though every nerve ending in his body was suddenly electrically charged. He'd seen so much over the years. *Done* so much. He frowned at that stray thought, then let it go. He was what he was. Too late now to regret the past. And far too late to beg forgiveness of a God who'd written him off a century before. But there would probably be a welcome party in Hell just for him. Grayson closed his eyes, smiled a little and waited for the flash of fire that would consume him.

"Are you all right?" A soft voice, definitely female, filled with concern and just a little fear.

He didn't have to hear her fright. He could smell it. Taste it. Opening his eyes again, though it took a Herculean effort, Grayson stared up at a woman, backlit by the growing light.

She smiled, shook her head until her short brown cap of curls danced and answered her own question. "Of course you're not all right. You're lying in the snow, probably half-frozen and your head's bleeding. Not a good sign at all."

His head was bleeding? Explained the pounding in his skull, but damned if Grayson could remember what had happened to him.

Her scent flavored the air around her. Soap and shampoo and something that was inherently *her*.

"Well, I can't just leave you lying out here in the snow." She stood, and looked around, as if hoping help would appear. When nothing happened, she glanced back at him and said, "I can get you out of the cold, but no way can I lift you. I probably shouldn't move you at all, but you'll freeze to death here, right?"

She nodded, convinced by her own argument. She glanced around the empty yard, then back to him. "The barn's closer. We'll go there, then figure out how to get you into the house. I can't leave you out here. And don't worry. I'm stronger than I look. I'm pretty sure I can drag you there."

Drag him? He glanced at her and with a single look took in her short, curvy figure. Dressed in a heavy sweater, blue jeans and boots that came almost to her knees, she was a slight woman, nowhere near muscular enough to drag him anywhere.

But she stalwartly grabbed his hands in hers. "Wow, you've been out here a long time. Your hands are like ice."

"Don't," he said, pushing that single word past lips that felt wooden, stiff with both the cold and the coming dawn. He didn't want her help. Didn't want to owe her anything. Safer for her if she just stayed away from him. He was a lost cause, anyway.

"You're right." She dropped his hands, and bent down in the snow beside him. "Look, I'll never be able to drag you. But I could probably help you walk, if you've got it in you. Just lean on me and we'll get you out of the cold."

She pulled him into a sitting position and Grayson, understanding that she was clearly not going to give up on helping him, called on every last ounce of his remaining strength. His body was tired. Fatigue seeped into every cell and bled into his veins.

The dawn crept nearer and every minute that passed brought him closer to oblivion. He'd thought, only moments ago, that he was ready to face it. That he welcomed the end. Now though, he felt the same will to survive that had trapped him in this particular hell a hundred and fifty years ago.

He leaned heavily on the woman and her scent teased him—surrounded him. He heard the rush of blood through her body and the fast gallop of her heart and everything within him hungered. Raw, desperate need formed a knot in his throat and Grayson choked on it.

His hand tightened on her shoulder and he steeled himself against the hunger that clamored to be eased. It had been a long time since he'd fed from a living human being. But damned if she wasn't a tempting morsel.

"Just a little farther," she said.

The sun was coming.

He stumbled and her arm around his waist con-stricted as she took more of his leaden weight. "Keep going," she said, her voice a whisper now, strained with effort. "Almost there."

Why did she care? What made her go out of her way for a strange man? Shouldn't she have been more concerned for her own safety rather than his? If she'd been smart, she would have called the police when she first spotted him. Although, if she had, he would have been no more than a pile of smoking ash by the time they arrived.

One more step. And another. He forced his legs to move. Forced himself to survive. Again. *Why?* Instinct, he guessed. Had to be. Even his kind fought for another day at life—such as it was.

He felt the skin on the back of his right hand sizzle. He glanced down and saw the slight twist of smoke lifting from his flesh as the first, barest hint of sunlight touched him. Grayson clenched his teeth against the searing pain and told himself it was no more than he deserved.

"Something's burning," she said, never slowing, never stopping. "Close by."

Yes. Closer than she thought.

He slumped against her as the sizzle and heat began on his cheek now. Exposed flesh, too long denied the sun, went up as kindling and Grayson knew he was only moments from being engulfed. And if the flames took him while she was wrapped around him, this Good Samaritan would die along with him.

He couldn't have that.

He'd done damage enough in his too long life already.

Pushing free of her, he staggered forward.

"What're you doing?" She tried to grab him again, but he lurched ahead, aimed at the open barn door.

"Stay back." Two words, delivered as an order not to be ignored. Then he lunged for the cool shadows within the barn and toppled into them once past the threshold.

Instantly, relief poured over him like the cool kiss of ice. The darkness swallowed him, and Grayson felt his body begin to heal, begin to awaken now that the morning light had been beaten back. He stirred, scraping his right hand on the rough wooden planks beneath him, and hissed in a breath as the rawness of his flesh erupted with pain. He cradled that hand in his other one and half turned to look at the woman standing in a slice of growing daylight. He squinted at her, made sure he was completely in the shadows, then said, "Thank you."

"You're welcome."

She didn't come any closer and Grayson wondered if she were already regretting her good deed for the day.

Bracing her feet, she crossed her arms beneath her breasts, tipped her head to one side and said softly, "Now, why don't you tell me who you are and why you're here."

"I'd like to know the same thing," he said, rather than answering her question. "I thought no one lived here."

"No one did until a few months ago," she said. "Now I do, and I still want to know why you're here."

Wincing a bit, he sat up and moved to one side, where he could brace his back against one of the stalls lining the old barn. In a split second, he took in the whole structure, noting that the barn was empty but for a minivan, a riding lawnmower—and, wouldn't you know it, there were a few slivers of growing daylight slanting through the gaps in the roof shingles. He nearly hissed at the sight, but managed to contain himself. When he looked back at her, he could see more than concern on her features. Her deep blue eyes were worried. Almost haunted.

He knew what that felt like and in spite of the situation, he almost felt sorry for her. Almost.

"I used to live here," he said.

"Really?" She didn't sound convinced. "Because when I bought the place several months ago, it was in good shape, but still looked as though no one had lived here in forever."

True enough. But he'd come here every year at Christmas. To be *alone*. Clearly, his business manager had decided to sell the old place and hadn't even thought to tell Grayson about it. The man deserved to be staked for this.

"It was a long time ago."

"Uh-huh." Still not convinced. "So why're you here now?"

He fingered the back of his head, pleased to see that the bleeding had stopped, though there was a knot there to remind him of how he'd come to be lying in the open. And now that the sun was no longer a threat, his memories of the night before got clearer.

"I got here last night. Saw the lights and was going to leave." He'd been pretty pissed off about it, too. He'd decided to spend the night in a nearby cave, but before he could leave, he'd sensed something in the woods. Not a vampire. But someone, watching the house.

When whoever it was had left, Grayson let them go. Vampires weren't big on playing the hero, after all. But then... "Someone hit me over the head. Next thing I knew, you were standing over me."

Her eyes went wide and frightened. "Did you see who it was?"

"No." Irritating as hell to admit that. His extraordinary senses should have warned him that he wasn't alone. But he'd been so damned surprised to find his home occupied that he hadn't paid close enough attention to the rest of his surroundings.

Tessa Franklin shivered and rubbed her hands up and down her arms. Frightening enough to find a nearly unconscious man in her front yard at the crack of dawn. But knowing that someone else had been sneaking around her house in the middle of the night was downright terrifying. What if he'd found her? What if he was watching her right now?

She hunched her shoulders against unseen eyes and fought for the calm she'd worked so hard to find. Pushing her fears back, she raked her gaze over her unexpected guest. A tall man, he was thin, but she'd felt the strength in him as he'd leaned on her moments ago. He wore black jeans, worn boots, a gray sweater and a short, black leather coat. His features were sharp, as if carved from stone with an ax. His eyes were dark, like his hair, his nose was long and narrow and his mouth was thinned into a grim slash.

Even injured, he carried an air of power that was nearly intoxicating—even to a woman who knew better than to trust a handsome man.

Still, if she were to guide her life by past mistakes, then she would have nothing. She had to move forward. Had to trust herself, or she would never be free.

Tessa looked into his deep brown eyes and said, "Look, you're hurt. So you can stay here for a while, if you want."

One dark eyebrow lifted. "You make a habit of inviting strangers into your home, do you?"

"Actually, yes," she said, forcing a brave smile she didn't quite feel. "I do. I run a B and B here. I've got one guest now and another arriving tomorrow, but I do have one more empty bedroom, if you need it."

He scowled at her. "I'm fine here."

"In the barn."

"Yes."

Odd. But then what about this morning hadn't been odd? "But you're injured."

"I'll heal."

She didn't know whether to be pleased or not with the fact that he clearly didn't want to come into her house. There was something about him that felt...dangerous. And Lord knew, she'd had more than her share of danger already in her life.

But she also saw something else in his eyes. An old pain that she responded to. How could she not recognize suffering in someone else? How could she not do everything she could to help?

"You can't stay in the barn," she said, deciding on the spot to insist on taking care of the man. She'd once needed help desperately and she was going to pass on that favor now. "You'll freeze out here."

"I won't be staying." He crossed his feet at the ankles and absently rubbed at the back of his right hand.

Tessa moved closer. "What happened to your hand? And your cheek?"

He blew out a breath. "I appreciate your help but I don't need further assistance."

"At least you could tell me your name," she said.

He was quiet for a long moment, then said, "Grayson Stone."

"I'm Tessa. Tessa Franklin." She held her hand out toward him and waited patiently for him to take it.

When he finally did, and his skin met hers, Tessa felt a jolt of something she couldn't identify pass between them. He felt it, too. She saw the flash of surprise in his eyes before he had the chance to disguise it. And somehow, it made her feel better to know that he was no happier about that flash than she was.

Moving farther back from her, he said, "I'll rest here, then move on tonight."

"Maybe that would be best after all," she whispered, still feeling the hum of her skin where he'd touched her. Her body was awakening to sensations she'd blocked for five years. And the raw ache within threatened to bring her to her knees.

She stood up and backed away, as if distance from this mysterious man could make everything she'd felt drain away. It didn't help. Shaken, she paused at the doorway, stood in the spear of sunlight and looked at him over her shoulder. Even in the shadows, the fire in his eyes burned hot. She felt the heat of him reaching for her and Tessa knew that Grayson Stone was more dangerous than she'd first believed.

Five years ago, she'd vowed to never give a man power over her again.

Up until this moment, she'd never doubted her ability to honor that vow.

Chapter 2

Tessa poured coffee into a thermos, gathered up a blanket and her first-aid kit, then carried it all back to the barn. Her one guest, Joe Baston, had spent the night in town, visiting his daughter. Joe hadn't wanted to put his daughter out—so he'd taken a room at the inn and so she had no one to make breakfast for and nothing to do except care for the man in her barn.

"What are you thinking, Tessa?"

Muttering to herself didn't really help, but it had become a habit during the last few years. Before coming to Whisper, Wyoming, she hadn't dared to make friends. Hadn't even stayed in one spot for longer than two weeks at a stretch. She'd kept moving. Always wary. Always scared, damn it. Until she'd finally awakened one morning to decide that she was through looking at life through her rearview mirror.

So she'd found this place, worked like a dog to fix it up and now she was running her own business. True, it wasn't much of a business yet, but that would change. All she needed was time.

Her stomach jittered uneasily and Tessa paused long enough to slap one hand to it in a futile attempt to calm herself. "Don't make this a bigger deal than it is," she said quietly, glancing at the barn just steps away. "He's hurt. You're going to help. Then he'll leave. End of story. Everything back to normal."

Except, just what *was* normal? She ran a B and B with only one guest. She lived on the outskirts of a town where she was still pretty much a stranger. Christmas was a week away and she was more alone than ever. And she hadn't had sex in five years.

Normal?

By whose standards?

"Sex? Who's talking about sex?" Taking a breath, she picked up the first-aid kit again and said, "You are, Tessa. And you should just cut it out now, got it?"

But who could blame her? The man in her barn, even injured, oozed sex from every pore. One look into those dark eyes and any woman with a pulse would want to throw herself at him. Tessa was no different—despite having plenty of reasons to know better. Completely disgusted with herself now, she headed for the barn before she could find an excuse not to.

The sun was up and slanting across the yard, glinting on the snow brightly enough to make her squint just to keep her eyes clear. Another storm was due, and judging by the thick clouds surrounding that clear spot where the sun clung stubbornly to the sky, it was going to be a big one.

The air was icy and every breath felt as though she were sucking knives into her lungs. The naked branches of the trees surrounding the house were draped in ice that looked like diamonds, dazzling in the sunlight. From a distance, the sound of a fast-moving creek came to her and Tessa paused again, just to enjoy the place she'd finally decided to call home.

Five long years of belonging nowhere, of owning nothing. Five years of using false names and never trusting a soul. Then one day, Tessa had driven down this lonely stretch of road, spotted this house and recognized *home*. She hadn't expected it. Hadn't really been looking for it. But this spot, this place, had called to her. As if it had been standing vacant, just waiting for her to come home and bring it to life again.

The small miracle was, that as she'd brought the old Victorian back from its slumbers…the house had awakened *her,* too. It was as if she was finally becoming the woman she'd once been. The woman who danced in the kitchen. The woman who could enjoy a quiet moment in the stillness, just appreciating a beautiful day.

And because she'd found that miracle, she was strong enough to help a man who looked as though he could use one, too.

With that thought firmly in mind, she headed for the barn again. Her boots crunched in the snow and the wind whipped around her, sneaking icy fingers down the collar of the jacket she'd thrown on over her sweater.

She didn't care though. It felt good to be alive. And if she was a little nervous about the stranger in her barn…it was a natural kind of nervousness. So that was good, too.

She rounded the corner, stepped through the open barn door and stopped. He was gone.

"Mr. Stone?" She took another step and now her boots clacked and echoed against the old wooden planks. "Mr. Stone."

"Over here."

Her head whipped to one side and she spotted him, all the way into the corner of the barn; he had his back to the wall and his gaze on her. All around him slivers of sunlight peeked through the roof like golden bars of a cell, holding him in place.

A niggling, ridiculous notion tugged at the back of her mind for a second before she could dismiss it. "Are you all right?"

"Great." His voice was tight. "Your roof needs fixing."

"Yeah, but it's low on the list right now." She walked toward him with slow steps. Funny, but she felt almost as if she were trying to ease up on a hungry tiger. He had a taut stillness about him that made her think of a predator. And that was almost enough to make her back out of the barn and leave him alone. But if she did that, then she would be surrendering to her own fears and she'd worked too hard to get past that time in her life. To rediscover her own courage and the spirit that had once been so completely crushed.

"Look," she said, forgetting about the fact that just a few minutes ago she'd wanted him gone, "you don't have to stay in the barn. I told you, you can come inside. It's warmer there and the roof doesn't sprout sunlight every few inches."

He scraped one hand across his face, then focused his gaze on her. Even in the shadows, she saw the flash of something molten in those dark depths.

"You don't have to do this." His voice rumbled out around her, soft, deep, almost hypnotic. "You should go back inside. Don't come back here."

"This is *my* barn," Tessa reminded him. "Of course I'm coming back here."

He groaned and let his head fall back against the wall behind him. "You have no sense of self-preservation at all, do you?"

"Excuse me?" She knelt on the floor beside him and opened the first-aid kit. "I'm not the one who was lying unconscious in the snow."

"I appreciate what you did, but you should just go back to your house. I'll be gone by nightfall."

"To where? I didn't see a car out front." And as she said it, Tessa wondered just how in the heck he'd come to be in her yard, anyway. Had he walked from town? In the snow?

"That's not your concern." He moved farther from her, tucking himself deeper into the shadowy corner.

Just then, the sun slipped behind a bank of clouds and the barn darkened, the slanting bars of sunlight winking out as if they'd never been. And the man huddled against the barn wall sighed, as if in relief.

"More snow's coming," Tessa pointed out with a glance behind her at the open barn door. She could smell it on the wind and in a heartbeat, she made a decision. "You can't leave. This storm is supposed to be a big one. You probably wouldn't make it into town before it hit—even if you had a car."

Scowling, he gritted his teeth and gave her a short nod. "You're right. I'll wait out the storm."

"Not out here, you won't." She picked up the first-aid kit again and stood up, to look down at him. "You'll freeze to death."

"You're not going to leave me alone, are you?"

"So I can find your frozen dead body in the morning?" She shook her head. "I don't think so."

"Fine." Grayson pushed himself to his feet and swayed a little, reaching out one hand to the wall to steady himself.

He was hungry. Every cell in his body cried out for blood and the temptation of having her so near to him was one he was hard put to ignore. Her eyes stared up at him with concern, though, and that was enough to at least momentarily bank the bloodlust clamoring inside.

She had helped him. He wouldn't repay her by sinking his teeth into her lovely throat.

No matter how much he longed to.

He shot a quick look at the world beyond the barn and noted that the light was gray, clouds having obliterated the sun. He could make it to the house. And once inside, away from the light, he could gather his strength. Then he'd leave her before his hunger outstripped his sense of chivalry.

"Lean on me." She wrapped one arm around his waist, tucking her shoulder under his arm.

"This is getting to be a habit," he muttered and was rewarded by the smile she flashed him.

"Let's get you into the house."

They made it across the yard and up the steps, with Tessa supporting his every stride. It had been a long time since Grayson had needed *anyone's* help. And accepting that help didn't come easily to him. Still, he didn't have much choice. If he didn't get into the house and away from the danger of sunlight, he would die. And just at this moment, with Tessa's scent filling him, he realized that he wasn't ready to march into hell.

"Come on," she said, opening the door. "Come inside and sit down near the fire."

Her invitation was enough to let him pass the threshold and he stumbled through the kitchen with her help, into the wide living room where a fire blazed and crackled in the hearth. She eased him onto an overstuffed sofa crowded with colorful pillows and Grayson laid his head on the back of the couch. The fatigue seeping into every square inch of his body dragged at him.

He hadn't been awake during daylight hours in decades. Now he remembered why. He battled unconsciousness, his thoughts becoming fuzzy, his breathing slowing. The scent of cinnamon hung in the air and mingled with the pine garland strung across the mantel. Christmas.

Not a particularly festive time in a vampire's year. Especially for him.

Being in this house again brought back memories so vivid, so alive, the empty room seemed to throb with them. He'd built this house himself. Moved his wife and children into it. Planned to live, grow old and die within its walls.

Well, he'd gotten one out of three right.

"Are you hungry?"

He turned his head to look at her. His gaze locked on the graceful column of her throat and he would have sworn he could actually *see* her pulse pounding there. Her blood would be warm and rich and sweet. He could almost taste it, flowing down his throat, slaking his thirst, easing his pain.

Deliberately, he closed his eyes. "No."

"At least let me get you some coffee."

"Fine. And—" he spoke quickly as she turned to go to the kitchen "—I'm expecting a delivery this afternoon. If I'm...asleep, will you sign for it?"

"Sure, but—"

"Thanks." That one word was a dismissal and she obviously felt it. He wasn't about to explain about the delivery of blood for which he'd arranged before he knew his house would be occupied. And, he told himself, his business manager was going to pay for it as soon as Grayson returned to New York.

"Okay, be right back."

He listened to the fire, letting its soothing sounds settle over him. Memories crowded his mind as sleep dragged him down—images of a different place, a different time, danced through his mind, one after the other. He allowed them to fill him and welcomed the pain as he remembered the faces of his children. His wife's voice.

Then the images shifted, changing, becoming the living nightmare that was never entirely gone.

His family's screams echoed over and over again in his mind and Grayson jerked awake suddenly with a shriek erupting from his own chest.

The sun.

"Damn it!" He jolted from the couch and the wide beam of sunlight lying across it.

The windows were uncovered to welcome whatever winter sunlight made it through the clouds. And the once shadow-filled living room was now bathed in a golden light that had already burned patches of skin from his hands and face.

Skin smoking, eyes streaming, Grayson took one long leap and stood against the far wall, air wheezing from his lungs. His fangs exploded in his mouth and the adrenaline coursing through him turned him into a dangerous creature. Age-old instincts rippled through him and whatever there was left of the man he'd been drained away. He was now a wild thing—looking for survival above all else.

"Fool." The day had made him slow and stupid. He should have secured the damn drapes. Made certain that no sun could reach him. But he hadn't been thinking. He'd been so wrapped up in the past he'd forgotten about the present.

He squinted into the sunlight streaming through the window and screaming pain lanced through his mind and body. His chest felt tight, his lungs strained for air. His skin was ablaze with burning agony. He turned his gaze from the window, lifted one scorched hand to protect his eyes and spotted Tessa, who had stopped dead in the doorway.

As if in slow motion, she dropped the coffee cup she held. It shattered on the floor, brown liquid splashing up on her jeans. Her eyes wide, her mouth open, she looked at him and he knew exactly what she was seeing.

A monster.

Chapter 3

"Oh, my God!" She clapped one hand to her mouth and stared at him through horror-stricken eyes. "You…who…*what* are you?"

His lips peeled back from his fangs and she shrank back another step or two. Caught against the wall, splayed there as surely as if he'd been chained, Grayson watched her and focused only on her. He couldn't allow her to panic.

He needed her.

A part of him was sorry to see that look in her eyes. A part of him had enjoyed being treated as an ordinary man. Yet, he didn't have time for her fear. He had only moments before the encroaching sun found him in the narrow patch of shade he stood in.

Staring directly into her eyes, he used the full force of his legendary power to direct her to do exactly as he ordered. "Go to the bookcase," he said, his voice tight against the pain still lancing through him. His fangs retracted slightly, reacting to the agony sweeping through him. Hissing in a breath, he swallowed back the pain. "There's a latch. Halfway down the first shelf. Pull it."

She did, taking one small step after another, as if she were a marionette and someone else—he—was pulling her strings. She found the latch, gave it a hard yank and the bookcase pulled away from the wall with a loud creak from the hidden hinges. Tessa only stood there, watching him, and Grayson couldn't allow himself to think about what she was feeling.

The only way to safety lay through the slanting rays of golden light. More pain. But then, pain had become a way of life for him. Pain and hunger. Both of which jolted through his system, leaving him both ultra-alert and exhausted. Gathering what little of his strength remained, he braced himself for the dash through sunlight into the promised sanctuary of the hidden room—hopefully without bursting into flame.

He bolted quickly and in four long steps, he was safely in shadow again. His skin buzzing, his hair smoking, Grayson took a breath and bit down hard on the agony holding him in a tight fist. He stood in the room he'd created for his family's safety so long ago and thought it ironic that this room hadn't served its purpose until he was dead.

Then Tessa, free of his influence, came around the edge of the bookcase and gave him a hard look.

Her breath was coming in short, sharp gasps, her eyes still shone with the shock of a truth she could barely believe and the scent of fear wafted from her like a heady perfume. But there was more. There was also anger.

"You lied to me."

He hadn't expected that to be the first thing she said to him. "I didn't lie."

"You let me believe you were a man. But you're not."

"No."

"You're…" Tessa broke off, unable to say the word her mind kept screaming.

"A vampire," he finished for her. "Yes."

"That's impossible." Tessa fought against the wild panic clutching at her heart, squeezing her throat tight until she felt as though she'd never draw another breath.

But even as she tried to deny it, she knew it was true. She'd seen his…*fangs*. God. Her head felt as if it were going to explode. She couldn't believe this was happening. There had to be some other explanation. Trick of the light. Her eyes went weird on her, that was all. She'd seen something that wasn't there.

Vampires only existed in television shows. Really gorgeous vamps, with souls who didn't bite people. Well, she told herself with another shocked look at him. He had the gorgeous part down pat. Who knew about the biting. Oh, God. A vampire.

This was so not happening. Clearly, the years on the run had pushed her over the edge. Her brain had finally snapped and who could blame her?

"Impossible," she repeated firmly, determined to not go believing in imaginary creatures—no matter how gorgeous they were.

"Is it?" He lifted both hands and she saw the burns marking his skin. Brain whirling, she remembered the same scorch marks she'd seen on his skin earlier, when she'd found him lying in the dawn.

Sunlight.

"No way," she said, fingers tightening on the bookshelf until she wouldn't have been surprised to see indentations from her grip smashed into the heavy wood.

He blew out a breath, scraped one hand through his thick hair and slowly stalked the confines of a hidden room she'd been completely unaware of. She kept her gaze on him, and still managed to give the small room a quick once-over. There was a square table and four chairs. A single bed pushed against one wall and several empty shelves along another. It was a safe room of some kind, she thought as he spoke again.

"Believe me or don't. That's your business."

He sounded tired. And she could understand that. Nearly going up in flames was bound to take a toll. Even from across this distance, she saw the scorched, burned flesh on the backs of his hands and on his face. He had to be in terrible pain, but he showed no sign of it.

And despite the evidence in front of her, Tessa argued with the only possible conclusion. She fixed her gaze on him and found the tattered threads of her courage. "Vampires don't exist."

"Not if you don't want them to." He leaned against the empty shelving and blew out a breath.

"If you are one, and I'm not saying you are," Tessa hedged, "why didn't you bite me before?"

He gave her a long, thoughtful stare. "Thought about it." His gaze lowered to the base of her neck. "Still thinking about it."

Her stomach turned over and fear quickened within only to dissipate a moment later. He'd had ample opportunity to kill her, but he hadn't. Instead, he'd warned her off. Tried to make her leave him alone. And right now, he was trying to scare her into backing away.

"You're lying again." She shook her head. "If you'd thought about biting me, you would have."

"No," he said with a smile that curled her toes. "I'm not lying. I wanted to drink you."

She sucked in air like a drowning person and felt the world tilt at a weird angle. As he stared at her, she could almost feel his mouth at her throat and a part of her wondered desperately what that would feel like.

Was he *making* her feel like this?

"Why didn't you then?"

Wincing, he rubbed one hand with the other and shrugged. "You were trying to help. Seemed ungrateful."

"A polite vampire?" Why did that sound so much weirder?

He laughed shortly, used the toe of his boot to pull out one of the ancient chairs and dropped onto it as if he didn't have the strength to stand any longer. Bracing one arm on the table, he leaned back, kicked his feet out in front of him and crossed them at the ankles. "Let's say old habits are hard to break. Good manners being one of them."

"I can't believe this is happening."

"I told you to leave me alone."

"You didn't tell me *this* though."

"You wouldn't have believed me anyway," he pointed out.

"True." She wouldn't have. If he'd been honest with her, she'd have thought he was crazy. She could hardly believe his truth now, and she'd seen the evidence with her own eyes. He had *fangs,* for Pete's sake. Sunlight had burned him. Another moment or two and he would have died. But, could someone already dead actually die again?

Who would ever have guessed she'd need the answer to that question?

"So now what?" she asked. "I mean, now that I do know, what're you going to do to me?"

"Nothing," he muttered and slapped one hand against the table.

"Why should I believe that you're not planning to bite me?"

"Because I give you my word."

"Uh-huh…" Her disbelief colored her voice. She'd heard promises before. And in her experience, promises weren't worth the breath used to make them.

"Stay in the sunlight," he told her. "Then you won't have anything to worry about."

"Until night."

He speared her with a look. "Look. I'm tired. I'm hungry."

She flinched.

He saw it. "You're right to be careful. I'm a vampire. Definitely not to be trusted. But you're safe from me, Tessa. I won't harm you. And I'll leave." He closed his eyes. "Just as I told you I would. Right after sundown."

Strange, but that assurance didn't make her feel any better. Oh, she believed he wouldn't bite her. She wasn't sure why she believed, but she did. It was his promise to leave that she didn't like. She wasn't sure why, but the thought of him disappearing from her life was not something she wanted to think about. Staring into his eyes, she saw pain and resignation and regret and felt those same emotions tugging at her.

He didn't speak again. And Tessa studied him. Without the fangs, he looked like any other man. Better-looking than most though, even with the patches of raw, angry skin on his face and hands.

Every instinct she possessed told her she could trust him. Foolish? Maybe. But she'd learned the hard way to trust her instincts.

They'd kept her alive when her would-be boyfriend had tried to kill her. Those same instincts had led her to this tiny town in Wyoming where she'd found this place and some small semblance of peace. And, they'd led her into the early morning snow to save this vampire's life.

There had to be a reason for it.

Before she could change her mind, she turned for the kitchen, grabbed the first-aid kit and headed back to where she'd left him. His eyes were open…those dark, penetrating eyes that seemed filled with a strength and a loneliness that drew her to him in spite of his warnings.

Deliberately, she took a step out of the sunlight and into the small room that was filled with shadows and the powerful presence of a wounded vampire. His eyes narrowed on her as she walked closer to him.

"I can't decide if you're foolish or brave," he said at last when she stopped alongside the table. "You're taking quite a chance, Tessa."

She held up the kit before setting it onto the table. "You're hurt. I can help."

"Why would you want to?"

Good question. Her fear was still rattling inside, twisting her stomach into tight knots. But here she stood, alone with a vampire. "Because I've been hurt and alone."

His gaze narrowed. "You should get the hell away from me."

"Yeah, you said that already."

Quicker than she could see, he shot out one hand, grabbed her arm and curled his fingers into her skin. The move was so startling, she jerked back despite her best intentions. He saw it and released her.

"You're afraid. I can smell it on you." One corner of his mouth lifted and fell in a blink. "To a vampire, that scent is compelling."

Her arm tingled where he'd grabbed her. His

eyes caught and held her and while she watched, the darks of his eyes bled into the whites until all she could see was her reflection shining back at her from the depths of twin black pools.

"You're a tempting package, Tessa." His gaze swept up and down her body with the intimacy of a touch.

"Now you're deliberately trying to scare me."

"Damn right." He straightened up in his chair. "Don't mistake me for some wounded hero. I'm a monster."

"No." Tessa looked at him and shook her head. "You might be a vampire, but you're not a monster. Trust me on this. I've seen a real monster. Up close and personal. You're nothing like him."

His gaze narrowed on her. "I'm not a man, either. The man I once was, died a hundred and fifty years ago."

She opened the first-aid kit. "How?"

"What?"

"How did you die?" She picked up the tube of antiseptic lotion and unscrewed the lid.

"Doesn't matter." He shook his head and glanced around the tiny, windowless space.

"Okay. How'd you become a vampire?"

He glanced at her.

"Same question," she said with a shrug. "Sorry."

"You're not reacting the way I would have

expected you to." He looked at her and while he watched her, his eyes softened, becoming again the dark brown they'd been when she first found him.

"More screaming, fewer questions?"

"Frankly, yeah."

"Well, here's another one for you," she said. "How'd you know this room was here? I didn't and I've lived here for six months."

"I built this room. Hell," he added on a short, humorless laugh, "built this house."

"Really?" She picked up one of his hands and tenderly smoothed some of the lotion onto the reddened, already healing skin. Apparently, he didn't need her help.

As if reading her mind, he said, "We heal fast."

She put the lotion away and closed the kit with a snap. From the other room, she heard a door open and a man's voice call out, "Ms. Franklin?"

Grayson snapped a look toward the sound.

Tessa grabbed the first-aid kit. "It's my guest, Joe Baston."

"He can't know I'm here."

"Yeah. I figured that out on my own."

But in a few seconds, Joe would be entering the living room and he'd see the bookcase pulled away from the wall. Quickly, Tessa spun to leave the hidden room. She paused at the opening to look back at Grayson. "You'll be safe here."

She stared into his eyes as she swung the bookcase closed, sealing her vampire in, and she wondered if she could say the same thing about herself.

Chapter 4

Grayson woke up in the dark. Nothing new there, but for a second he couldn't figure out why he was awake. He sensed that it was still daylight because his body hadn't recharged itself yet. The lethargy bore him down into the flattened, hundred-and-fifty-year-old mattress on the narrow bed he'd constructed so long ago.

His burns were mostly healed, but his hands still tingled with the reminder of the close call he'd had. Hell. He hadn't been caught in daylight since he'd been newly changed. One day with Tessa Franklin and he'd almost become a torch.

Twice.

When the cell phone in his pocket rang again, he realized what had pulled him out of sleep. Grabbing the damn thing, he checked caller ID, then answered—only because he knew this caller wouldn't give up until he'd gotten through. "What is it, Damon?"

"Where the hell are you?"

Damon St. John, the Vampire King, wasn't known for his patience in the best of times. With his new reign already threatened by lesser vampires looking to take over, this was clearly not the best of times.

"None of your business," Grayson told him. "I'm out of this and you know it."

It was a long-running argument. Damon and he had been friends until Damon had decided to take an active part in governing the vampire "community." Now, he'd been named king, but there were factions that weren't happy about Damon being in charge.

Grayson didn't care. He stayed out of politics, and instead kept to himself, along the way earning a reputation as being a rogue. Which was fine by him. He'd spent the last hundred years keeping a low profile. He'd amassed a fortune out of hard work, luck and, hell, boredom. And the king was counting on Grayson to back him in the fight to keep his throne.

"You're in Wyoming, aren't you?" Damon's disgust came clearly across the phone. "Still punishing yourself for surviving?"

"Back off." Grayson sat up, bracing his elbows on his knees. This was an old argument, too. Damon had never been able to understand why Grayson hadn't simply accepted being a vampire. The freedom. The immortality.

Maybe it was because his immortality had come at too high a price.

"I need you back here."

"You've got plenty of support," Grayson reminded him.

"The other side is counting on you," Damon said tightly. "They figure if you're not supporting me, you'll be on their side. Are they right?"

Pushing himself off the cot, Grayson stalked around the small, dark room. Outside, there was a world going about its business. Here, there were only shadows. And memories. He shoved one hand through his hair. "No," he said. "They're not right. I'm out of this."

"That's where you're wrong," Damon told him. "You can't be out. You're a vampire. And it doesn't matter how often you go to that damned house of yours. You'll never be a man again. So why don't you just let it go? Move on?"

"Stay out of this, Damon." Anger simmered inside.

"Fine. Torture yourself some more. Just keep your eyes open. Seems my enemies are looking for you."

When they hung up, Grayson tossed the phone

onto the old table. Hell, maybe Damon was right. What was the point of coming back here year after year? Maybe his business manager had done the right thing in selling off the house. Maybe it was time he accepted who and what he was.

He threw a glance at the back of the bookcase as if he could see beyond that doorway into the house where Tessa was. She'd surprised him. Intrigued him. And he wanted her. Wanted the taste of her in his mouth and the feel of his body inside hers.

Everything in him itched to find her, toss her onto that damned cot and have her. Instincts he'd been at war with since his change rose to the surface and shook him to the bone. Tessa Franklin had thrown him. Hard.

Then he remembered what Damon had said. Other vampires knew about his habit of coming to this house at Christmas. If they followed him here, Tessa wasn't safe. He'd brought the vampire war directly to her door.

His chest tightened. If another vampire showed up on her door, she wouldn't suspect him. She'd probably think he was just another guest for her damned inn. Which meant she wouldn't be able to protect herself.

Which meant he was going to have to do it for her.

Looked like he was involved in this vampire war whether he wanted to be or not.

"Definitely time to stop coming here," he muttered and sank down onto the chair.

Tessa had a vampire stashed in a secret room, but that didn't keep her from attacking Christmas week in a big way. She busied herself hanging more garland and setting out the cranberry- and pine-scented candles. There was a dish of chocolates on the living room table that she dipped into a little too often, but since she had a vampire in her house, Tessa figured she was due a little extra chocolate.

Besides, staying busy kept her from thinking too much. Thinking about how her vampire had once owned this house. Heck, *built* this house. About the power in his eyes. About what it felt like when he'd touched her.

And he's not your vampire, she told herself firmly. For God's sake. A vampire. She couldn't stop thinking of that word. Obsession. Good sign. But she couldn't help the way her insides jangled when she thought about him.

She *had* to stop thinking of the word *vampire*.

Which was why it was a good thing that her only customer, Joe Baston, was checking out early. He was a nice man, but Tessa couldn't help but be grateful that he was leaving. Hiding a vampire in your secret room was a lot easier when there wasn't anyone else around.

Vampire.

Stop it! Her fingers shook as she filled in the credit card slip for the older man standing opposite her. Giving him a smile she hoped he wouldn't notice was a little too forced to be really cheerful, she said, "I hope you come back, Mr. Baston."

"Oh, that'd be real nice. It's a great place you have here." He glanced around at the high, beamed ceilings and the fresh cream-colored paint on the wood plank walls. "Homey. Welcoming. I think you've got yourself a winner with this inn."

Not if all of her customers left as early as he did, Tessa thought but didn't say.

But he seemed to understand, since he spoke up again quickly. "I'm sure sorry about leaving early." He didn't look sorry, though. His pleased grin was infectious. "But my daughter's insisting I stay with her while I'm here, and it's a chance to spend lots of extra time with the grandkids."

"It's not a problem, really," Tessa said, watching him sign the slip. After all, she'd only been open a couple of weeks. She was sure to get more customers after the holidays. "I'm glad you're enjoying your trip."

"Well," he said, tossing the pen onto her desk, "I'll be sure to tell folks what a nice place you've got here."

"I'd appreciate it, thanks." Tessa smiled and waved as he headed out the door, and then she looked around the empty room.

She needed more Christmas in here. A tree, of course, but one glance at the snow currently pelting the front windows told her that she wouldn't be taking care of that chore today.

But she did everything else she could think of—pausing every now and then for a glimpse at the bookcase hiding Grayson Stone from her.

Amazing how much the world could change in twenty-four hours. God, yesterday seemed like a lifetime ago. Yesterday, she hadn't even known vampires existed. Now she had one stashed in her house.

Was she crazy?

Probably. Absolutely, who was she kidding? Vampires were fictional. Dreamed up by authors trying to scare gullible readers when everyone knew there were enough scary *real* things out there already!

The doorbell rang. She jolted out of her thoughts and hurried across the room. She peered through the glass in the upper half of the door and spotted a private delivery van in the driveway. Opening the door, she was slapped by an icy wind and wet splats of snow. Squinting, she half hid behind the door and asked, "Yes?"

"Delivery for Grayson Stone." The short guy in a beige uniform and a fluorescent orange parka held out a clipboard with a sign-in sheet and a pen attached to it. "Sign at number sixteen."

"Right." Grayson had told her a package would arrive. She signed her name, handed the clipboard back and when he turned to leave, she saw the box on the porch. Plain brown wrapping and a name and address label. No clue to what was inside.

She fought the wind, grabbed the box and stepped back into the house, slamming the door with her hip. The fire crackled and hissed as she stared down at the box and wondered about what could be inside. Carrying the heavy parcel across the room, she pulled on the bookcase latch and let the doorway swing open.

Grayson grabbed her at the throat.

She yelped, dropped the box and he let her go instantly. Staggering back, Tessa gulped in some air and forced her heart out of her throat and back into her chest where it belonged. She flipped her hair back out of her eyes and glared at him. "What the heck was that for?"

"Announce yourself. I didn't know who the hell might have discovered this room," he muttered, moving to the table.

"So you had to strangle me?" She rubbed her throat and could still feel the strength of his grip imprinted on her flesh. "Besides, even *I* didn't know this room existed. How's a stranger going to wander in and discover it?" Fear dribbled into the pit of her stomach, despite the fact that he'd let her go as soon as he'd figured out that she wasn't a threat.

"Sorry." He paced to the far wall, spun around and looked at her.

He kept a safe distance from her now, as if to convince one or both of them that he wasn't going to hurt her.

"I'm not used to being around—"

"Humans?" she finished for him.

He nodded. "Yeah."

"Well, try harder." She waved a hand at the toppled box. "The package you told me about was just delivered."

"Good. Thanks." He walked to it, picked it up and set it onto the table. Then he looked at her meaningfully.

She frowned. "What is it?"

"Mine."

Tessa shook her head. "I want to know what's in my house."

He watched her for a long second or two, then gave her a sharp nod. Tearing the strapping tape free, he opened the box, lifted out a Styrofoam packer containing dry ice, then reached deeper. He pulled out a small, plastic bag filled with…blood.

The thick red liquid sloshed back and forth while he held it and Tessa's stomach did a quick pitch and roll. Of course. Vampire. Blood.

"Okay…" She pulled in a breath and let it go again slowly. "I just…I guess I wasn't expecting to see that."

"Vampire, remember?" He dropped the blood back into the box and folded his arms over his chest. "I've got connections at a blood bank."

"Wow. 'Blood bank' sort of takes on a whole new meaning for me now."

He frowned at her. "It's better this way, believe me. I haven't drunk from a living human in nearly a hundred years."

How insane was it that she actually found that information sort of comforting?

As if he sensed her relief, he added, "That doesn't mean things can't change."

"You're deliberately trying to keep me scared," she pointed out. "And not that it's working, but why?"

"Because you should be." He came around the table, laid both hands on her shoulders and pulled her closer to him. "Others of my kind know I come here every year. Some may come looking for me. That means you're not safe."

"*More* vampires? *Here?*" Looking up into his deep black eyes, she shivered. "Why are they looking for you?"

He let her go and shook his head. "There's a war brewing in the vampire world. We're expected to take sides."

"A vampire war?" Tessa's voice sounded strained

even to herself, as if she'd had to squeeze those words out a too tight throat. "And it's coming here?"

"Maybe." He scraped a hand across his jaw. "I don't know who's coming—hell, even if anyone *is* coming. Can't be sure."

"And if they do come, then what?" The small dribble of fear she'd felt earlier became a running river, pushing through her veins, making her mouth dry and her head feel light.

He slanted a look at her. "If they come, then you should be gone."

Go? When she'd finally found a home? When she finally had something to live for? A chance at a life that wasn't revolving around hiding? No.

She'd run before to save her life.

Now she would stay to fight for it. "I'm not leaving."

"Yeah. Thought you'd say that." Walking back to the table, he reached into the box and picked up a packet of blood. "So. Looks like I won't be leaving tonight after all."

"Damn straight," she snapped, fear giving way to resolve at the thought of hordes of vampires descending on her. "You can help me make stakes… and I wonder if the church in town is open. Holy water. A bucket or two full. And…" She stopped, looked at him and said, "I know why I want the help. But why are you volunteering to stay?"

"Because I brought this here. And I'm not going to bring more death into this house."

His gaze was dark, his features tight and every square inch of him looked poised for battle. That sense of power that clung to him filled the tiny room and practically hummed in the air.

"*More* death?"

"A hundred and fifty years ago," he said quietly, "my wife and children died in this house. And I was the one who invited their killer inside."

Chapter 5

Grayson ignored the stamp of curiosity on her features. He'd said more than he'd planned and now regretted it. But then he was used to a life filled with regrets. What was one more? Lifting his head, he reached out with the finely honed senses of his kind and smiled. "Near sundown."

"Close. But it's snowing, so there's no sun anyway."

"You have a microwave?" he asked, picking up a packet of blood and leaving the rest in the shipping box. He headed out of the secret room, not waiting to see if she followed. He'd had more than his share of small spaces crowded with too many ghosts for one day.

"Of course," she said, coming up right behind him. "Why do you...oh."

He stared at her, then deliberately lowered his gaze to her neck. "I prefer my blood *hot*."

She swallowed hard, but she didn't flinch this time—just stared right back at him and he had to give her points for it. All in all, Tessa Franklin was a woman who could adjust to the bizarre fairly quickly. A shame she wasn't more careful.

If more of his kind showed up here looking for him, it was likely they wouldn't show her the same sort of consideration he was. They'd look at her and see her only as something to drink.

Why that bothered him more than it should, he didn't care to think about.

He walked back to the kitchen and waited while she got him a coffee mug. He smirked at the happy face stamped on it in bright yellow, but opened the packet of blood and poured it inside. Opening the microwave, he set the mug inside, closed the door and punched the timer.

While he waited, he turned to look at her in the overhead lights. Beyond the kitchen, the day was dying in a swirl of ice and snow. He saw trees bending with their heavy white burden and heard the moan of the wind as it curled around the house.

He focused more sharply then, and heard the skittering footsteps of a small animal looking for shelter. There was a brush of something more, too. Not vampire. Not completely human. Something— it was gone as quickly as it had come. Had he imagined it? Was he so primed for a threat, he saw one where none existed?

He shook his head and heard the buzz of the light fixture, and the beat of Tessa's heart. That quick, staccato rhythm told him she was more nervous than she pretended to be.

Courage or foolishness?

His mind still open to any possible threat, he reached into the microwave when the timer dinged, took out the mug and had a sip.

She frowned, but he ignored it. "We all need blood to survive, Tessa. Even humans."

"Yeah." She blew out a breath and looked him square in the eye, as if trying to tell him she wasn't bothered by the sight of him drinking. "I guess you're right. It's just—"

"Easier to take with an IV tube?"

"Yes."

"I am what I am. Have been for too long to apologize for it now."

"I didn't ask for an apology."

Not with words. But he read her eyes. Those deep blue eyes that looked at him and saw a man—

until he reminded her otherwise. He shrugged and moved to the bay window overlooking the yard and the stand of woods beyond. Changing the subject because he preferred talking of things that didn't matter, he said, "It hasn't really changed much over the years. You say you just bought it."

"A few months ago." She came up beside him with quiet steps. "The first time I saw the house, I knew I wanted it. It was as if it had been sitting here. Waiting for me." She reached out and touched one hand to the mist on the cold window, leaving her fingerprints in the damp. "Sounds silly, but I felt like I'd found home."

"It's a good place," he said, not commenting on her little confession. But he knew what she meant. He'd felt the same when he first saw this piece of land so long ago. It had all been wide open then. With the nearest neighbor almost twenty miles away. He and his family had settled into the seclusion and hadn't minded being on their own.

Until that last night.

As if she knew his thoughts had turned to the past again, she spoke up.

"What happened? I mean…"

"I know what you mean." He took another drink of the hot blood, savoring the thick, rich taste as it slid down his throat. Appropriate, he thought, that he should have blood in his mouth to tell this story.

"It was Christmas night." His voice was cool, detached, as though he were talking about something that had happened to a stranger. And that was more right than not, after all. It had been so long now, the man he'd been had nothing to do with the person he'd become. "A man came to the door. Freezing. Hungry. So near death I thought he wouldn't last the night. I brought him inside."

He remembered it all so clearly. The scents. The sounds. The baby's cry, his wife's soft humming, his son's laughter. Decades fell away and Grayson tumbled into his own private hell. "We warmed him. Fed him. Though it wasn't food he wanted."

He shifted his gaze to hers and held it, trapping her in the story with him, dipping into her mind, so that the pictures he painted were as vivid for her as they were for him. "He killed my wife first. One twist of her neck and she was gone. I fought him, but he was too strong. I remember seeing murder in his eyes and I recall the feel of his fangs as they sank into my neck. Then the next thing I knew, it was morning and I wasn't dead. Though everyone else was."

Seconds ticked past before she swayed, closed her eyes briefly and said, "Oh, God. Grayson…"

"He could have killed me, too, of course. Instead he turned me. So that I'd wake and find what he'd left behind. So that I'd survive, knowing everything I loved was dead."

"You couldn't have known. When you brought him into the house—you couldn't have known."

He refused her offer of sympathy, brushing it aside as if he hadn't heard the shock and sorrow in her voice. "That's the point I'm trying to make to you. No one can know. You run an inn. Do you think vampires never stay in hotels? You think they really do live in caves and sleep in coffins?"

"Up until I met you, I didn't know they existed!"

"Exactly. You don't know. You wouldn't recognize a vampire if it came to your door." He laughed shortly. "Obviously. You didn't recognize the danger in *me*. Instead you let me in. You wanted to take care of me."

"You see compassion as a weakness," she argued. "It's not."

She still didn't get it. Grayson felt a surge of anger rise up inside to nearly choke him. She couldn't— or wouldn't—see the danger around her. Which meant she was in even more jeopardy than most.

"You're the kind of person vampires live for. Most of them are just killers. They're not interested in making others of our kind. All they want is to feed and destroy. They leave a trail of misery behind them and think nothing more of it once they've moved on. It was blind, stupid luck for you that I've sworn off humans. Otherwise—" he paused for a sip "—let's just say you'd make a damned good snack, Tessa."

Her eyes narrowed.

In a blink, he set the mug down, grabbed hold of her arm and gave her a hard shake. "Not everything out there deserves your compassion, Tessa. You don't want to see what's out there, that's your business. But until I'm sure that none of my kind have followed me here, you'll listen to me. You'll open your eyes. You think you're prepared. Safe. But you're not. Humanity thinks it knows evil, but none of you have a clue."

He held her tight with one hand and waved the other toward the window and the storm beyond the glass. "There are creatures moving among you that live only to cause pain. Who look for nothing more than the opportunity to strike. Do you think you can fight them off? Do you think you can survive?"

Her breath came fast and furious. She pulled free of him and he saw fire in her eyes when she glared at him. It pleased him. At least she had a temper and knew what to do with it.

"You think you've got the patent on suffering? Someone killed your family and left you to live with the memory?" She slapped both hands to his chest, gave him a vicious shove that didn't budge him in the slightest. Even more furious now, she shouted, "You think you're the only one? You're my first vampire, but you're nowhere near my first brush with real evil. Big deal. Vampires bite. Humans kill, too, you know...."

There was something raw in her eyes now. A bleeding pain that ripped through her and reached out to touch him as well. He refused to acknowledge it.

"But a human is still something to be reasoned with," he told her.

She laughed at him, the sound harsh and ragged. "You think so?" Her short dark hair dropped onto her forehead and she tossed her head, sending it out of her way. "I ran for *five* years from a man—a *human*—who said he only wanted to love me."

She couldn't stand still. She walked in jerky steps to the kitchen counter and back again. "God. He really believed that, too. Two dates. That's all we had. Two dates and my instincts told me to get away. I knew there was something wrong with him. Something terrifying. So I broke it off."

She sent Grayson a look that was filled with bone-chilling terror. "He wouldn't listen. He stalked me. Haunted me. He stood outside my house at night, followed me to work in the mornings. I got a restraining order." She rubbed her arms viciously as if her blood had congealed in her veins. "That only made him madder. He set fire to my car. He killed my dog. Finally, he broke in to my house when I was out and killed a friend of mine who picked the wrong night to stop by with pizza...."

Tears streaked down her face, unheeded, unchecked. Her eyes were wild and furious and filled with a pain he recognized, as he lived with something much like it every day. He reached for her, but she jumped back from him.

"Don't." Tessa held up both hands and fought for control. God, she'd shatter if he touched her. She knew she would. Cold wrapped itself around her entire being, squeezing her heart, icing her lungs until she felt as though she might never draw another breath.

Her memories were every bit as emotionally charged as his. She couldn't go a single night without dreaming of the past. Without seeing her home, her things shattered, Jamie's broken body laying splayed and forgotten in her living room. She heard over and over again the quiet calm of the policeman's voice. The flash of the red and blue lights on the squad cars slicing through the darkness.

She felt it all. Remembered it all. And had finally found the courage to live anyway. To forge a life for herself. To refuse to surrender to the terror Justin had subjected her to.

She'd escaped. That was what she clung to. What she had to keep uppermost in her mind. She'd finally found a way to stand in the light. And she wouldn't go back into the darkness.

Looking at the man across from her, she stared into his dark eyes and wondered why she'd opened up to him. Wondered how Grayson Stone had become so important to her in such a short amount of time. How he'd gotten past the defenses she'd erected so carefully around her heart, her emotions. He was a stranger. He called himself a monster.

But somehow, he was so much more, too. She took a deep breath, blew it out and said, "Just don't touch me right now, Grayson. I don't want your sympathy. I don't even know why I told you that. There's something about you, I guess—I don't know. It's just…I don't like being treated like I'm an idiot. I'm not." She met his gaze. "I've already survived a monster and I'll do fine with whatever else comes at me."

The organ that had once been Grayson's heart twisted for her sake and the sensation was so rare, it startled him. It had been a century or more since he'd cared about anything. Or anyone.

Why now?

Why her?

"I'm not running anymore," she said as if expecting him to tell her to leave again. "Like the saying goes, *Been there, done that.* I changed my name so often even I couldn't keep track of who I was at any given moment. I lived in dumps. Rooming houses or cheap motels. I didn't have friends. I supported myself with temporary jobs because I was too afraid to even use my savings, for fear he'd somehow track me down that way. All I thought about was keeping my head down. Hiding. Running."

She shook her head, used her hands to swipe away what was left of her tears, and then she lifted her chin, pride making her spine straight. "Until I came here. I found this place. And it's mine. It's *home*. I'm not going to run again. Not because of him. Not because of you. And not because of some vampires that may or may not show up."

Grayson watched her, saw her determination, her strength, and though he admired her for those traits, he knew they might also get her killed. "You're not going to listen, are you?"

She inhaled sharply, forced a smile she didn't feel and shook her head. "No, I'm not. Besides," she offered as her smile took on a touch of warmth, "it's nearly Christmas. I escaped my own personal nightmare on Christmas Eve. So I'm a big believer in Christmas miracles."

"Miracles." Even the taste of the word felt foreign to him. Especially since her "miracle" time of the year had been an ending for him. He'd prayed that night, fast and desperate. But nothing had come to save his family. To prevent the destruction of everything he loved.

Yet, hadn't she survived her own trip in to hell? And she'd come out not only whole, but with a strength of purpose that humbled him. Grayson studied her and fought the rising tide of sensation inside him.

She touched something in him. Something he'd thought dead and buried long ago. And he wasn't sure whether to be grateful or furious about that.

But either way, Grayson knew he wouldn't be leaving until she was safe.

"So," she said after a couple of long minutes, "if we're finished with the true confession portion of the evening, how about you help me string some lights around the front porch?"

He blinked at her. "Lights?"

"Yeah." She grabbed her jacket from a hook by the back door and slipped into it. "Sun's down—or nearly anyway." She smiled and grabbed the doorknob. "And as long as you're here, you can help."

Standing in the open doorway, Grayson stared after her, with the wind and cold slapping at him. Hanging Christmas lights hadn't been part of his plan in coming here. But things had changed.

He shifted his gaze to the woods that straggled around the edge of the property and studied the shadows. His senses were honed, and as he searched, he reached for that brief flash he'd felt earlier.

But it was gone.

Chapter 6

Grayson strung lights. He hung up an ornament-and-pinecone-studded wreath on the front door and even helped wrap wide, bright, red ribbon around the columns along the porch.

He shook his head as he slipped through the night, amazed at just what he'd come to. Putting up Christmas decorations, for pity's sake. He still wasn't sure exactly how Tessa had managed to get him to help. But one look into her deep blue eyes and he'd heard himself agreeing to all manner of things he wouldn't have considered before.

Glancing back at the house, he paused a moment to take in the jewel-like brilliance of it. Lamplight shone from every window. The twinkling, multicolored lights ran along the bottom rim of the roof and smoke lifted and twisted from the chimney.

It looked like a Christmas card.

Scowling to himself, he turned his back on the festive sight and loped into the shadowy depths of the stand of woods. He found the snow-covered duffel bag with his clothes easily enough. He'd dropped it when he was hit on the head the night before. Grabbing the icy leather strap, he swung his gaze over his surroundings, searching for that hint of something wrong.

He'd felt it earlier. Then again when Tessa was laughing at him over the placement of her damned ribbons. Something. Someone? In the woods.

Watching.

Who was being watched, though?

Him? Or Tessa?

Thoughts of her brought Tessa's image to mind and he wanted to growl at himself for giving a damn about what happened to her. It wasn't only hearing her story of the man who'd stalked her. It wasn't the fact that she'd saved his ass by dragging him out of the encroaching sunlight. It was more. It was *her*.

By rights he should have been gone by now. Far away from her and what she made him feel. But damned if he'd walk away wondering if he'd left her in the middle of a vampire war. Swinging one arm back, he tossed his duffel toward the house and listened for the muffled thump when it landed. He'd pick it up later. When he came back.

For now, he'd had enough of close proximity to Tessa. He needed to be in the night. Where he belonged. Where he didn't have to think about a human woman who was spending far too much time in his thoughts.

A snap of sound caught his attention and Grayson instinctively dropped into a crouch. Swiveling his head, he focused his mind, his senses…and waited.

From the house came the soft sounds of smooth jazz playing on the stereo. Further away, the rushing water in the river chuckled as it rushed past rocks. A dog howled in the distance and a car's engine gave a muffled roar. He heard it all. Felt it all. He was connected to everything that moved in the night, every small heartbeat of rabbits and squirrels resonated in his mind and became part of the symphony of sounds he sifted through with deliberate calm.

And finally, he felt what he searched for. A faint brush of something that didn't belong here tickled at his mind and Grayson smiled. He dipped beneath a low-hanging pine branch and didn't even react when a dollop of snow dropped down the collar of his jacket and shirt, sliding along his spine.

He'd spent most of the first decades of his eternal life hunting in wilderness much like this. He knew all too well that silence and stillness were his best weapons. Even as a human he'd been a woodsman. And since his change, he was able to move even more soundlessly.

A twig snapped again to his right and he had to wonder if his quarry were truly that clumsy or simply trying to trap him.

Then a scream ripped through the night.

"Fire! Grayson, fire!"

He bolted, forgetting about quiet, not caring who heard him moving through the trees. An unfamiliar surge of protective fury raced in his blood and brought Grayson hurtling from the woods into the clearing just beyond the house.

Light flickered over the snow. Lamplight. Christmas lights. And the dancing, shifting light of the fire already eating away at the barn door.

It sounded like a hungry dog, all growls and snaps.

Tessa was sprinting toward the barn and Grayson charged after her, slamming into her body and carrying them both into the nearest snowbank. He broke their fall, then rolled her over and stared down into her eyes.

"Stay away from the fire," he warned in a growl that sounded as fierce as the flames themselves.

"Screw you," she said and gave him a shove, pushing herself up out of the snow. "It's my barn, I can help."

Rather than argue with her, Grayson ran for the barn doors. The flames were quick but they hadn't been burning long. They licked at the dry wood and leaped upward in the soft night wind. But those ravaging flames were still small enough to be beaten back with some of the snow that lay so handily around them.

Grayson kicked at the thick white stuff, spreading it in wide arcs over the flames. Hisses and thick black smoke were his reward as those wicked orange and yellow lights died. Again and again, he sent snow toward the fire and when Tessa ran up and joined the fight, the two of them had the danger smothered and steaming in just a few minutes.

The stench of blackened wood was raw in the air, yet beneath that heavy scent, there was something more. The faintest trace of gasoline. Grayson's gaze narrowed thoughtfully on the woods before shifting to look at Tessa.

Her face was as white as the snow drifting down onto her dark hair. She wasn't wearing her jacket and when she shivered, she seemed almost surprised.

Grumbling, he pulled her into his arms and scrubbed his hands up and down her back. "Adrenaline's wearing off. You're freezing now."

"Wasn't. Before." Her teeth chattered, which was hardly surprising, since she was wearing only jeans, a long-sleeved shirt and a pair of furry, pink, soaking wet slippers on her feet.

"First a fire, next pneumonia," he muttered, wondering how in the hell this human woman had become *his* responsibility.

"Fine." She said it again. "I'm fine. Fire out?"

"Yeah." He looked over her head at the blackened bottom of the barn door and thought about just how quickly the whole damn thing could have gone up if she hadn't noticed the flames in time. Anger roared to life inside him as he held her trembling body against him. Feeding the rage nearly strangling him, Grayson let his gaze swing around the empty yard and the woods beyond.

He felt it again.

That brush of something dark against his mind. Whoever their watcher was, he was back.

He wanted to race after the arsonist. Track him. Find him. Drain him dry for putting that glassy look in Tessa's eyes. For bringing fear to a house and a woman who'd seen too much of it already. But he couldn't leave her to make her way inside alone.

"Come on. Inside." He turned for the house and felt the sharp stare of hatred boring into his back like a knife. The watcher in the woods didn't like him much.

Which suited Grayson just fine. He didn't like hunting a friend.

* * *

Tessa couldn't stop shaking. From her toes to the ends of her hair, she'd never been so cold. She felt as if her bones might shatter.

Grayson laid her down on the couch near the fireplace and she curled into herself, wrapping her trembling arms around her knees. He covered her with a colorful afghan and brusquely rubbed his hands up and down her back, her arms.

She felt sensation come crashing back as her skin seemed to prickle with the stabs of a thousand needles. "God," she whispered, dipping her mouth beneath the edge of the blanket. "I'm frozen."

"Hardly surprising." Grayson stood, lifted her wet, bedraggled bunny slippers and let the melting ice drip from the toes onto the rug. "Why the hell would you go into the snow wearing these ridiculous things?"

She scowled at him. Well, her eyebrows drew down and she narrowed her eyes at him. She was too cold to pull her face out of the blanket to snarl. "I wasn't thinking about the cold. I saw the fire and—"

"Panicked?"

"Reacted."

He tossed the slippers to the stone hearth, where the beady bunny eyes stared at her in reproach. The heat pouring from the fireplace was so comforting—and yet, only moments ago, another kind of fire had been the enemy.

"The whole barn could have gone up," she said, watching the flames instead of staring up into dark eyes that made her tremble even harder than the cold.

"I think that was the idea."

She looked at him. "What?"

"I smelled gasoline."

"I didn't," she argued.

He nodded his head. "I can pick up scents others might miss."

"Handy talent," she murmured. As her limbs began to warm, she struggled to sit up. "But who would burn down my barn?"

"That's the question, isn't it?" He folded his arms over his chest and looked down at her. "What about your stalker? Could he have found you?"

Another wave of cold swept over her as Tessa considered that possibility. She'd been so careful. So diligent about keeping a low profile. It had been five years. Surely, Justin wasn't still fixated on her. And even if he were, he wouldn't be able to find her. Not here.

But even as she thought it, she had to admit, even to herself, that she couldn't be sure. "I don't know. God, I hope not."

Grayson went to a corner cabinet, picked up a bottle of brandy and poured some of the honey-colored liquid into a snifter. Walking back to her, he handed it over and said, "Drink it."

"I hate brandy."

"Drink it anyway."

She took a sip, and though she disliked the taste, had to admit that the resultant heat zipping through her bloodstream was more than welcome.

Still, she made a face when he said, "Finish it."

While she stoically sipped at the brandy, he dropped into a crouch in front of her, bringing their eyes to the same level. Staring at her, he said, "There's another possibility."

She nodded, hardly able to believe what she was about to say. "A vampire."

"Strictly speaking, we tend to steer a wide berth around flames…." One corner of his mouth lifted briefly, though that tiny half smile didn't go anywhere near his eyes. "We're more combustible than humans. But it's still possible that whoever set that fire is my enemy—not yours."

She didn't want to think about another vampire being in the woods, watching her, her house. But the only other option was to consider that Justin had found her again. And she didn't think she could bear to live through another onslaught of Justin's "devotion."

She was alone out here. The only help she had, the only man she trusted…was a vampire.

The false heat of the brandy swam through her system, but her body trembled anyway.

Not with cold.

With fear.

Chapter 7

For the next two days, Tessa walked around in a sort of fog. She baked and cleaned and decorated in a determined frenzy designed to keep her fear at bay.

But it was always there. Just under the surface. She stepped out onto her porch and wondered if someone—Justin—was out there looking back at her. When her phone rang, she jumped. When a car backfired on the road, her heart jolted. When the college student who'd arrived the night before surprised her in the kitchen, she had shrieked and dropped a pan of cinnamon rolls. Her nerves were strained to the breaking point and there was no way to ease the tension.

She'd lived with fear for so long that feeling it wrap itself around her now was like meeting up with an old enemy.

Chilling, yet somehow familiar.

And her vampire bodyguard—who would have ever thought she could say those words?—scarcely left her alone. Well, except for those hours when he was trapped within the secret room. But even then, she felt his presence. His *power,* reaching for her. As if even in his absence he was letting her know she wasn't alone. And she wondered what exactly she would do when he left. How would she live without being aware of him? Without feeling him in some corner of her mind? Her soul?

There was a deep, undeniable connection between them, though Tessa couldn't understand how it had started. And she knew it couldn't end well. She was human. He wasn't. She would eventually grow old and die and he would still look as he did today.

As he had for more than a hundred years.

So why then, she demanded of herself, did she spend so damned much time thinking about him? Because, she thought, it was much more agreeable than considering the possibility that Justin had finally found her.

But it was more than that, too. Knowing Grayson was here gave her a sense of safety that she hadn't known in far too long. Which was weird in itself, when she thought about it. Having a vampire around shouldn't make her feel safe. And yet…

It was still the middle of the day, but the snow was falling in a steady sheet of white beyond the kitchen windows. According to the weather report, this new storm would be dumping up to two feet of snow by morning, and would effectively close the roads. Which meant the guests she had been expecting tomorrow afternoon wouldn't be arriving. So as soon as the college student upstairs checked out, her B and B would be empty, but for her and Grayson.

A chill swept along her spine and it had nothing to do with fear.

Little by little, she was losing her grip on the nice, normal world she'd built for herself. And at the moment, the only stable point in her little universe was a vampire.

How insane was that?

She'd begun counting down the daylight hours… waiting for sundown. Waiting for the moment when Grayson would step out from the secret room. He was probably sleeping now. And she imagined him stretched out on the narrow cot, the blankets lying low across his abdomen, his chest bare…

"It's a great place."

"Whoa!" Tessa jolted out of her daydream, convinced her heart to slip back down her throat into her chest and sucked in a gulp of air.

Standing in the open doorway to the living room was her one and only guest. Michael Chevron, college student, on a driving trip home to his family in Montana for the Christmas holiday. He stood about six-two, had blond hair and guileless blue eyes, and the smile he gave her was sheepish.

"Sorry," he said, holding up both hands. "Didn't mean to startle you. Again. Broke my heart when you dropped those cinnamon rolls last night."

Already moving toward the coffeepot, Tessa poured him a cup, waved him to the table beside the bay window and set the cup in front of him. "It's the weather, I guess. Makes me a little jumpy."

He grinned and swung a hank of pale blond hair out of his eyes. "Oh, I don't know," he said, with a glance out the window. "I like the snow. Keeps everything sort of dark and cozy. Quiet."

"Yeah. I guess so." She shot a look at the swirling snow beyond the window. "But you can only take so much dark."

Although, with the sun safely behind a thick bank of storm clouds, Grayson would be able to join her as soon as he woke up. That thought made her smile and worry at the same time.

Funny how much she'd come to depend on his company in just a few days.

And it wasn't only his company she wanted.

She recalled with perfect clarity the look in his eyes, the punch of sexual tension when he'd carried her inside after the fire. She could still feel the swirl of heat through her body, pooling thick at her center. How he'd looked at her while she lay shivering on the couch. She'd felt that hot, steamy stare of his right down to her bones. And if truth be told, she'd thought then that he was about to kiss her.

And she remembered all too well the disappointment she'd felt when he hadn't.

Strange how much she wanted him. She couldn't remember a time when she'd ever experienced such overwhelming need for a man. The fact that it had all happened so quickly was a stunner, too.

As if, somehow, it was meant to be.

"You okay?"

"Huh? What?" She shook her head and looked at the smiling, handsome face across from her. "Sorry. Guess my mind was wandering."

"Not surprising," he said, toying with the handle of the coffee mug. "When you spend so much time alone, your thoughts are bound to drift."

"I suppose so."

"You *are* alone here, right?" He gave her another smile. "I mean, I thought I heard you talking to someone late last night."

"Must have been the TV." She could hardly admit

to having a man stashed away in a hidden room, could she? "I'm sorry if it disturbed you."

"Oh, it didn't." He shifted a glance around the brightly lit room, then looked back to her. "I just thought there might be someone else staying here after all."

"Nope. Just me." Suddenly Tessa had a bad feeling. The young man's smiling face hadn't changed any, but there was something else. Something she couldn't quite put her finger on. Something that made her uneasy enough to stand up and move away from him.

She busied herself at the kitchen counter, wrapping up the fresh bread, all the while watching him from the corner of her eye. The ticking from the clock on the wall seemed overly loud. The snow slapped at the windowpanes and her own heartbeat sounded to her like a roar.

When he stood up lazily and stretched, she felt everything inside her tighten in expectation.

He carried his coffee cup across the room, set it down on the counter. Tessa tensed as he stood too close, and at the last moment she realized she couldn't feel any sort of body heat emanating from him. He was there. But it was as if he weren't real. As if he—

"Okay, enough already." He grabbed her, spun her around and backed her into the counter. Slapping his hands onto the counter edge on either side of her, he effectively trapped her in place. That affable smile disappeared and his eyes went from innocent to deadly in a blink. "I know he's here. Where?"

"He?" She choked out the single word and fought for breath. Something, she saw now, he wasn't doing at all. Breathing, that is. His blue eyes swirled with shadows, darkened, narrowed. He parted his lips and fangs appeared.

God.

"No more games." He leaned into her, pressing his body along hers, driving the small of her back into the counter's edge until pain screamed through her mind. "I know he's here. I sensed him this morning. He's sleeping. That's the only explanation for why he's not blocking his presence from me. So I'm going to ask you one more time…"

He dipped his head, scraped the tips of his fangs along her throat until she shuddered. Pain there, too. A burning sensation. Above and beyond the pain though, she felt the slow, steady dribble of blood down her neck that told her he'd broken the skin.

To prove it, he licked her throat, while she groaned and closed her eyes briefly against the horror of this moment.

Then he lifted his head and sighed. "Sweet. You taste so sweet. And your fear gives your blood that little kick I enjoy so much. Makes me thirsty for more." Taking one hand from the counter's edge, he reached for her hair, stroking his fingertips through it. "Now, this is your last chance. Where is he? Tell me and I'll go. Don't tell me and I'll turn you. Here. Now."

Turn her? Make her into a vampire? She still felt the daggerlike points of his fangs against her skin. And she knew that he wouldn't hesitate to bite her again, more thoroughly this time. But how could she tell him about Grayson? He was asleep. Defenseless. She couldn't.

Wouldn't.

Just as she wouldn't stand still and do nothing while she was threatened. Fear rattled her bones, but desperation had a stronger hold on her. Blindly, while he watched her, waiting for her answer, Tessa reached behind her on the counter. There was a knife close. She'd used it only moments ago to slice bread. Now her hand found it, her fingers curled around the smooth, wooden grip.

He grinned at her and his fangs glistened in the overhead light. "Ah, I see that light in your eyes. Stubborn, aren't you? I like that in a woman. Makes the chase more interesting. And, I was hoping you wouldn't tell me where to find Grayson. Good for you. Loyal and all that. Works out nice for me. I'll have you now and when I'm finished…when you wake…you'll tell me where he is. And we'll end him together before we…celebrate."

"I don't think so."

He laughed, delighted. "You think you can stop me?"

"Probably not." She stabbed him, shoving the bread knife deep into his side, and used that moment of surprise to bolt from the room.

She got as far as the living room before he grabbed her hair and yanked her back. Pain exploded inside her head and battled with the fear that ripped her breath from her lungs.

"Stupid bitch. Did you really think a knife would do you any good?" He gave her a furious shake, and looked down at the shirt he wore. "You ruined it. And though knives can't kill me, they hurt like hell. So I'm thinking you'll pay for that, too."

"Let her go."

Everything in Tessa went calm and still. Despite the pain still raging inside her. Despite the terror closing her throat. She heard Grayson's voice and felt safe.

Keeping a tight grip on her hair, Michael the vampire turned slowly around to face the man standing in the open passageway beside the bookcase. Michael laughed. "A secret room? How cool is that?"

He sounded so young, Tessa thought wildly. Young and excited…and so deadly.

"You came here for me. Let the woman go."

"Why should I?" Michael pulled her close and,

keeping one eye on Grayson, lowered his head to lick at the blood still seeping from her neck. "I think I'll have her. Once I'm finished with you, of course."

Grayson looked into Tessa's eyes and saw not only fear, but also a steady calm. Damned if he wasn't proud of her. He could taste her terror staining the air, but instead of weeping and wailing, she was doing all she could to hold herself together. And judging by the bloody tear on Michael's shirt, she'd done some damage, as well.

The voices had wakened him and as soon as he'd realized who was in the house with Tessa, he'd felt a fury he hadn't experienced in a century or more. To know she was in danger—because of him—was something he couldn't tolerate. Now, there was only once choice. To end Michael before Tessa was hurt any further.

"This wasn't necessary," Grayson said, walking slowly closer.

"Sure it was." Michael backed up, laughing, dragging Tessa with him. "If you're not with us, you're against us. And that gives the king too much power."

"I'm not with him, either," Grayson pointed out.

"A rogue vampire's nobody's idea of a good thing, either, Gray," Michael said easily. "You gotta take a stand. Our side or theirs."

The snowy light from outside fell in gray strips across the room. Lamplight puddled in golden circles and the hiss and snap of the fire in the hearth sounded like the curses of chained beasts.

One fist clenched at his side, Grayson kept his gaze locked with Michael's, and the chair rung he held tightly in the other hand hidden behind his leg. "If I have to choose, then I'll go with the king. He was elected after all."

"Yeah?" Michael laughed again. Boyishly. Charmingly. "We want a recount."

"Too late." When he was close enough, Grayson moved in a blur of speed. Lifting his right hand, he sent the chair rung hurtling toward Michael's chest. It struck home before the too young vampire had even felt the impact.

A split second later, the smiling boy with the demon's heart was dust.

Tessa dropped bonelessly to the floor and just sat there, stunned and shocked and shaking. Grayson was beside her in a heartbeat, running his hands up and down her arms, tilting her head to one side to see the puncture marks on her neck. Her blood, thick and red, pooled on her skin. He ripped the sleeve of his shirt, folded up the material and held it to her neck.

"Little bastard." The words were tight and fierce, though his hands on her skin were gentle.

"Scared me," she admitted. Leaning forward, she leaned her head against his chest. She blew out a long breath and took another before speaking again. "He turned on me so fast, I guess I wasn't really prepared. Glad you showed up when you did."

He checked her wound, satisfied that the bleeding had stopped, then wrapped his arms around her and held on, knowing instinctively she needed comfort. And that at least, he could give her. She sighed against him and he leaned back, against the wall, drawing her with him until she was curled into his side.

"More will come, won't they?" she asked, her voice quiet, hesitant.

"Probably."

She tipped her head back and he looked down into those deep blue eyes that haunted his sleep, tormented his dreams, made him wish for things he shouldn't have.

"Will you stay with me?"

"Yes. Until I can get this straightened out…be sure you're safe again. I'll stay."

"I'm glad of that."

He smoothed her hair back from her face. "You shouldn't be."

"You won't hurt me."

"If we go on from here, I'm bound to."

She caught his hand and he felt her warmth slide through him like a blessing. The feel of her in his arms was so right and so wrong all at once. He wanted from her things he couldn't have. Things he hadn't wanted for more than a century. Things he'd thought he was long since over.

There was a long, thick line dividing them. The line between life and death. That should have been enough to keep him from her.

But staring down into those dreamy eyes that watched him with stillness and trust, he knew nothing could stop him from having her. Hunger reared up inside him. Desire. A craving that caught him at the base of the throat and squeezed.

She reached up, cupped his cheek with her palm and steered his face down to hers. Cursing himself, knowing that he had no right to touch her, Grayson took what he needed anyway.

His mouth closed over hers and the demon within the man howled.

Chapter 8

The taste of her was more than Grayson had expected and far more than he deserved.

He wasn't gentle. Wasn't slow or kind or thoughtful. He surrendered to his own thundering need and she responded in kind. She didn't pull back, suddenly thinking better of the whole thing. Instead, she strained against him, pressed her breasts against his chest, and he felt the hard buds of her nipples like twin brands.

Her heartbeat thundered and her hands grabbed at him, his hair, his back, fingers curling into his shoulders as she held onto him and gave him everything she had. He was drowning in her. Feelings he'd buried rose up within him. All for her. All for the woman who looked at him as if he were a man. Those deep blue eyes tore at him, making him more and less than he was.

And Grayson needed her beyond anything he'd ever known. He blessed whatever Fates had sent him here, to the place where he'd died—to allow him to feel as if he lived again. Later, he knew, even as his body raged, there would be a price to pay. He would have to leave her and these exquisite feelings behind. To go back to the shadows and leave her in the light. But for now, this moment, she was his.

Terror slid into desire and heated together until Tessa's blood ran like a river of lava. She'd known from the moment she first saw Grayson Stone that they would, eventually, come to this.

His mouth on hers, his cold hands sweeping up under her shirt to stroke her skin, sending shivers through her body, filling all of the empty, frightened corners inside her. She tasted his need and fed it with her own. His tongue plunged into her mouth and tangled with hers.

Tessa arched into him, groaning tightly from the back of her throat. There was so much. So much more than she'd ever experienced. So much more to still feel. To still enjoy.

He made quick work of her clothing and in only

moments, she was lying on the rug naked. Outside, the wind screamed like a beast clamoring at the windows. At the hearth, the fire leapt and spat. But the world could have disappeared and she wouldn't have noticed.

She saw only him.

She stared up into dark eyes that sparked with the same kind of hunger racing inside her. She wanted his hands on her. Wanted him inside her, deep, so deep they would be somehow forever connected.

"Now, Grayson. Come to me now." She reached for him, both arms open in welcome.

He stripped so quickly his movements were a blur, and then he was there, sliding over her, covering her body with his. His skin was cool and yet, she imagined a kind of warmth in him. A warmth that reached for her despite their differences.

He kissed her. Her mouth, her cheeks, her jaw, her throat. He licked the spot where the vampire had bitten her, and instantly sparkles of fire, of pleasure, rose up within her, flashing through her bloodstream.

She sighed and held his head there, to that now so sensitive spot. "Again. Do that again."

He did, then scraped his teeth gently over her skin and she wanted him to bite her. To take away the fear of what had been done to her by giving her the sensual pleasure of knowing he drank from her. Knowing that he was taking into himself everything she was.

Her hands moved through his thick, silky hair while his hands caressed her breasts, thumbing her nipples until she felt the tingling response down to the soles of her feet. She was alive for him in a way she'd never been before. Every cell in her body was alight with sensation and as she stared up at the darkened wood beams overhead, she saw everything in a misty blur. She couldn't focus on anything beyond the feel of him atop her. The strokes of his hands, the feel of his mouth, still nibbling at her throat.

She twisted beneath him, her core hot and needy. She arched her hips in invitation as he lifted his head and looked down at her. Positioning himself between her legs, the tip of him just pressed against her heat, teasing, promising. And Tessa reached down between their bodies to stroke his hard, solid length.

He hissed in a breath he didn't need, but his gaze never left hers. Leaning in to her, he shook his hair back from his face and whispered, "This is a mistake, Tessa. You can still stop it. I'll walk away. For your own sake…tell me to walk away."

Tessa felt the power of her gender and knew the secrets that had been handed down from Eve to all those who had come after her. She saw his need for her flashing in his eyes and knew that one word from her and he would step back. He would go from her and what lay between them would dissolve into an unfulfilled memory.

Just as she knew she could never let that happen. Her hand fisted on him, squeezing, creating a pressure that made his jaw muscles twitch and his eyes slide shut on a sigh of pure pleasure.

"This is no mistake," she said, lifting her hips again, rubbing the tip of him against her heat. "This is meant to be. Now come to me, Grayson. Fill me."

"God help you then, because I can't." The words were a strained, taut murmur of surrender. She released him and he moved, sliding into her, spearing her with his length until he was buried so deeply inside her, Tessa would have sworn he was touching her heart.

He moved again and again, his rhythm increasing, his thrusts hard and fierce. Her heart leaped into a frantic beat as even her skin felt electrified by his touch. She went with him, matching his pace, caught up in the rush to completion. She wanted it all.

Sensation poured over her in a thick wave and her vision blurred until all she could see were his eyes. Dark, deep, fathomless, swallowing her.

He bent his head to hers, took her mouth with his, their tongues meeting, tasting. Her breath exploded from her lungs as she struggled with the tangle of raw feelings churning within. Her body lit up as she rode the crest of pleasure. She felt her insides coil tight, tighter. She ran her hands up and down his back, spread her thighs wider, hooked her legs around his hips and drew him even deeper inside.

There was so much. And still she wanted more. She wanted that most intimate of touches from him. Crazy. It was crazy. She knew that as a still rational corner of her mind whimpered, but she was beyond rational. Beyond logic. Trapped in a web of heat and desire that muddied her brain and demanded that she experience what only he could give her. With one hand, she steered his face to her neck. To the spot where the vampire had bitten her, terrified her.

Grayson's mouth worked her skin…his tongue, the tips of his fangs scraped her flesh and she shivered, holding him to her. She felt him stiffen.

"No," he whispered, his lips moving on her skin even as he held himself still inside her body. "I won't. I won't do that to you."

Turning her head, struggling for air, Tessa looked at him and whispered, "I want you to. I want you to take away that memory of what happened before and give me a new one. I want to give you what you need."

His features went to stone. "I don't drink humans. Haven't in more years than I can count."

"Drink me, Grayson. Just once. Just now. Drink me."

"Is that what this is about?" His gaze held hers and she felt him withdraw even though his body was still locked within hers. "Sleeping with a vampire?"

"No," she said, smiling. Her hand cupped his cheek. "It's *you*. I know you won't hurt me. I know you can't hurt me. And I want to feel you take me inside even as I take you."

He watched her, considering, thinking for what could have been forever, but was probably only moments. And then he drove his hips hard, thrusting deep. She groaned, tipped her head back, and her throat was laid bare to him.

Bare and beckoning.

"Grayson, take me."

She looked up at him, then guided his head back to her neck. Back to the spot that still seemed to burn from the bite of the vampire who'd wanted to kill her. "Take me, Grayson. Give me a memory to replace the one I have."

She felt him yield to her. Felt his acquiescence. And an instant later, his fangs pierced her flesh and her body went up in flames.

Ecstasy.

An instant of pain followed by the most exquisite delight she'd ever known. He drank from her, his mouth working at her flesh even as his body continued to buck into hers. Tessa's mind whirled with a dizzying blur of thoughts and images. They were one now, joined in blood and body, and the feeling was more intense than anything she'd ever known. He filled her. Heart. Mind. Body.

And Tessa cried out his name when her core exploded into a frenzy of incredible sensations.

A moment later, he closed the tiny wounds at her throat and climaxed himself, emptying everything he was into her.

Later, when Tessa thought she could move without shattering, she rolled to one side and curled into him. His arms came around her, his chin rested on top of her head.

"We've made things more complicated," he said and she heard his voice rumble from his chest.

"Yes." She tipped her head back so she could look at him. "More complicated, but I don't care."

He smiled briefly…more a twist of his lips than anything else and it was gone almost before she could enjoy it. "You will."

"Then I'll worry about it then." Sitting up, she looked at him and lifted one hand to shove her tangled brown curls back from her face. "I told you about the last five years of my life. How I spent most of my time scared…too afraid to stand still. So afraid of *losing* my life that I didn't really *live* my life."

"Yes."

"I'm done with that," Tessa said and felt a heavy weight lift off her heart. "I'm going to make decisions that feel right for me and not second-guess them. Today…a vampire almost killed me in my own kitchen."

He reached for her and stroked one hand down her bare arm. "That was my fault. I brought the danger here."

She covered his hand with hers and smiled. "That's not my point. I survived it. I fought back. And when it was over, I had the most incredible sex of my life with the vampire who saved me."

That too brief smile creased his face again. "Incredible?"

Tessa laughed and God, it felt good. "Figures *that's* the word you'd focus on."

"No. I'm focused on *you*." He sat up then and cupped her face in his palms. His gaze moved over her features, as if cataloguing everything about her in his memory.

Tessa's heart turned over as she realized that even now, in this lovely, glowing period after they'd shared so much, Grayson was, in his own way, preparing her for goodbye.

"You are…unexpected," he said, his eyes as dark as the night. "I didn't plan to take you. To be taken. But I cannot regret it now that it's happened."

She lifted her hands to cover his. "I regret nothing, Grayson. I don't want you to, either."

"One day, perhaps I will. But not today." Shifting, moving with a blur of speed, he snatched her up, drew her across his lap and held her cradled against his chest. Staring down into her eyes, he said, "What you are calls to me. Who you are stirs something inside me."

"I'm glad." Tessa had never felt anything like this before. This *bond* between them was electric. All-encompassing. And she felt as though she could stare up into his eyes for the rest of her life.

"You are the incredible one here, Tessa Franklin." His voice was like black silk. "I thank you for making me feel—however briefly—like a man again. But never forget," he warned. "I may look like a man, but I am not one. I am a vampire. And there can be nothing lasting between us."

Chapter 9

The taste of her still filled him two days later and the cravings for her hadn't eased. Grayson dreamed of her during the long daylight hours when he was trapped in that secret room. And the times when she came to him there, he lost himself in her, greedily taking what she offered, knowing that soon he would have to leave her. For her sake.

She couldn't form an attachment to him because there was no rosy future waiting for the two of them. He was undead. And she was so very much alive.

Disgusted with himself, he kicked at the snow under his feet and his boot sent a flurry flying into the ever present wind. This was why he rarely involved himself with humans. This was why he kept to himself. Caring about someone—someone mortal—was an invitation to pain. Their lives were so short, comparatively speaking, and watching as they aged and sickened and died—while he remained always the same—was simply not something he enjoyed.

And vampire friends were few and far between. Most of them cared only for the hunt and those that were different were more like Grayson and kept a distance between themselves and the others of their kind.

Tessa. Even her name brought a glow of something warm into the darkness he carried with him always. Standing here in the biting wind and the flurries of snow, he got hot and hard just thinking about her. They made love often, as if each of them had realized that their time together was nearly done. As if they both wanted to savor whatever pleasures they could in the time they had left.

The lingering flavor of her, the staggering realization of the trust she'd placed in him. The link between them, thick and shining. All of it was both gift and burden.

And Grayson hated himself for using her. For taking what she offered so freely. His honor demanded that he keep her safe—but damned if he could leave her alone.

The demon was gone, but the threat remained. Now Grayson knew for sure that the vampires were aware of just where he was. Now he was certain Tessa was in danger.

For the last two days, Grayson hunted at night, stalking the perimeter of the house, despite the sharp teeth of the storm that held them in an icy grip. Snow piled high, the wind shrieked under the eaves of the house, and in the shadows, menace still lurked.

He didn't sense a vampire, but since an older demon would be able to mask its presence as well as Grayson could, that proved nothing. There were stirrings of humans nearby, but he couldn't pinpoint a particular threat.

And so he watched. And waited. And stayed primed for a battle he knew was coming. He'd tried to contact Damon, the king, in an effort to get the dogs called off. But phone service had been affected by the storm as well.

It was as if they were cut off from the rest of the world, something he ordinarily would have enjoyed. But it wasn't only his own neck he had to watch out for now.

He stood, silent and still in the swirling snow, and stared at the house across the yard from him. The twinkle of the lights blurred in the blowing snow, but they shone on, despite the cold. Despite the threats. And he considered that Tessa was much like those lights.

In spite of—or maybe because of—the things she'd been through, she continued on. Unstoppable. Unquenchable. And the shadowy threads of the man he used to be stirred for her. She was amazing. She didn't allow fear to overpower her. Didn't allow her past to control her or make her decisions for her.

More than he could say for himself.

He scraped one hand across his face, turned away from the house and slipped into the trees. He had to stop thinking about Tessa. Had to stop pretending, even to himself, that he was the man he once was.

A scent twisted in the icy wind. He lifted his head as it shot past him and caught at his throat as he recognized it.

Blood.

Tessa screamed.

The deer had been viciously slaughtered and laid across the back porch.

Blood. So much blood.

A river of red poured over the whitewashed wood and dripped down the steps in tiny, determined rivulets. Even over and above the sound of the storm, Tessa heard the splash of each drop as if it were the beat of a drum.

She couldn't tear her gaze away. She couldn't stop looking at what had become of the doe. Her stomach lurched and spun. She swayed, looked down at the deer, its soft brown hide drenched in its own blood. And the smell of the kill rose up to fill her nose, her mouth, her pores. A sob choked her, trapped in her throat, and then Grayson was there, leaping across the porch to land beside her.

He turned her face into his chest and she let him. She couldn't look again. Couldn't face the death someone had brought to her home.

"I opened the door." She shook her head and inhaled the sharp, spicy scent of him to counteract the horror at her feet. "Was going to bring in more wood for the fire. I smelled it first. Smelled—"

"I know." He cupped the back of her head and held her to him. "I caught the scent only a moment before you screamed."

"So whoever did this...*just* did this." She inhaled and forced herself to stop trembling. To stop being so damn scared. "Which means they're probably out in the woods now. Watching me. Watching us."

"Yes." She felt him turn his head to stare past her, through the wall of white that blew past the house, into the stand of trees that bowed beneath the snow and offered so many hiding places. "I can sense something. Someone."

Tessa took a breath, steeled herself and said, "Vampire?"

"No. A vampire wouldn't have wasted the blood to make a point."

Wasted. Dear God.

She fisted her hands in his shirt and the chill of the snow clinging to him slapped at the panic inside her. "God. God," she breathed and didn't know if it was a plea or a prayer.

"Go inside." He turned toward the still open door and gave her a gentle push.

But she didn't move. Didn't want to step out of the circle of his arms. She wanted—needed—him close.

"A human did this, Tessa."

A human.

As if it were palpable, Tessa felt a sense of evil swell from the woods and reach for her. She shivered and Grayson's arms tightened around her. Death hung over the inn and Tessa knew that this was only the beginning.

A vampire had tried to kill her two days ago. And now a human was adding a new threat to the mix.

And she knew who it had to be.

Felt it in her bones.

"It's got to be him," Tessa said, pulling back from him, looking up into dark eyes. "It's Justin. Has to be. He's found me. No one else would have done this. No one else hates me this much."

His arms tightened around her middle like steel bands. His features went hard and cold and the darkness in his eyes swirled with the promise of vengeance. "He won't get to you."

It was a vow and she was glad to have it. Glad to have Grayson with her. Glad to know that he would stand with her. And desolate to know that once the threats to her were over, he would leave.

Deliberately, she put that thought out of her mind, and concentrated on the fear and the anger churning within her to make a combustible mix of emotion. She would not allow Justin to reign over her life again. She absolutely refused to become the terrified woman she had been before she had found this place. This refuge.

"Now, go in the house. I'll take care of this." He gave her a shove in the general direction of the open door, but Tessa dug her heels in.

"No." She pulled in a deep breath despite the stench of blood that clung to it. "I won't be the little woman, tucked away for safekeeping."

Grayson scowled—expecting the fierceness of his expression to be enough to get her following his orders. She sniffed and shook her head.

"Forget it. This is *my* house and nobody is going to drive me off. Not even you, Grayson."

He studied the deep, steady blue of her eyes and knew he was fighting a losing battle. "Stubborn women are a curse on all mankind."

"Ain't it the truth?"

He hissed in a breath he didn't need. "It's not safe for you to be outside."

"Grayson…" She laid one hand on his chest and he would have sworn he could feel the heat of her touch all the way through him.

"I'm not an idiot. I'm not thinking about racing out into the woods trying to track down whoever did this." She squared her shoulders and stiffened her spine. "I'm going to be right here. On the porch. But I won't be locked away as if I were a child."

He shook his head at her. In a hundred and fifty years, he'd never met another woman quite like Tessa. Her strength. Her pride. Everything about her was magnificent.

Despite the fact that she wouldn't listen to him. "Do you know that no one argues with me?"

She smiled and though her eyes were still shadowed, he saw a spark of humor glinting at him. "Well then, that explains a lot. It's not good for a man to think he's right all the time."

The wind kicked at them, spitting snow and tearing at her hair with icy fingers. He smoothed one curl back behind her ear. "You have nothing to prove, Tessa. Allow me to do this for you. This kill has sickened you."

She gritted her teeth together and completely avoided looking at the dead deer on the porch.

"Your face is white as the snow in the yard. Just being this close to the kill is making you sick."

"I know." She swallowed, lifted her chin and kept her gaze on his. "And the faster we get this taken care of, the faster we can get inside by the fire. Okay?"

He gave up. She wouldn't listen and maybe it was better all around if she were where he could keep an eye on her. "Fine, then. But let's be quick."

So he worked, carrying the deer off into the woods for the predators in the woods to finish off. As he moved, Grayson kept his senses on alert, constantly aware of his surroundings. The sounds of the forest, the heartbeats of the animals who slept in the snow. Whoever had left this carcass wasn't here now. There were no humans close by and if there were any vampires watching, they were blocking themselves from him.

He and Tessa were alone.

For now.

A couple of hours later, when the deer and the blood had been taken care of, and Tessa was in the shower, Grayson stood on the porch, looked at the woods and shouted a challenge.

"Come out of hiding, you bastard." His voice was iron and he pushed a command into every word. "Come out now and face me. Or are you only capable of terrifying women?"

His only answer…black waves of rage that rolled toward him in thick ripples. Grayson's hands fisted at his sides and a matching fury rose up inside him. Whoever lay in wait was able to resist the compulsion to obey him.

Vampire?

Or a human so twisted, so evil, that its mind was an empty well, devoid of the normal human emotions so easily manipulated by Grayson and others like him?

The wind moaned and though he strained to hear more, there was nothing. His enemy continued to hide, continued to evade him, and Grayson was fast losing patience. What he wanted to do was stride into the stand of trees and stay there until he found whatever threatened Tessa's safety. But he couldn't leave her alone to do the hunting every fiber of his body demanded.

It had been a century or more since he'd hunted humans. But as he stood on the porch, defying the cold, he knew that he would do whatever was necessary to defend the woman he'd come to care for far too much.

"Grayson?"

He turned to look over his shoulder at the woman waiting for him in the kitchen. Fresh from the shower, her pale skin was flushed, her tumbled curls still damp. She wore faded jeans and a long-sleeved red T-shirt that clung to her breasts and skimmed the curve of her waist. She shivered a bit in the draft of cold air sweeping into the house, and that was enough to get him to step inside and close and lock the door behind him.

She walked up to him, linked her arms around his neck and went up on her toes to plant a hard, lingering kiss on his mouth. When she finally pulled back, he saw that her eyes were still troubled, but she forced a smile to belie the shadows in those blue depths.

"Let's forget about whoever is out there," she said, smoothing her fingertips through his hair.

"That won't change anything, Tessa."

"Does it have to?"

"No," he admitted, pulling her close, burying his face in the curve of her neck so that he could draw in the scent of her and hold it deep inside him. "No, it doesn't."

Then he kissed her and the world fell away.

Chapter 10

Tessa wrapped her arms around Grayson and held on tightly. Parting her lips for him, she welcomed his demanding invasion and met his tongue with her own in a tangled dance of need and desperation.

What did it say about her life that the one thing holding her together was a vampire? She didn't know. Didn't care. All she was sure of was that the one person in the world she felt a connection with was the one person she couldn't have. Even while Grayson held her, she could feel him pulling away. Keeping an emotional distance when physical distance was impossible.

She knew he'd be leaving soon. Knew that when

he did, she would never see him again, and that knowledge tore at her.

His hands swept up, under her shirt, across her skin, lighting up every cell as if she'd been electrified. His hands slid down to the waistband of her old jeans and she took a breath and held it as his fingers undid the button and slid the zipper down. Then his hands were on her, cupping her behind, then sweeping around to stroke the heat of her sex.

She pulled her mouth from his, stared up into his eyes and watched him as he dipped first one finger, then two, into her depths. Tessa sucked air into her lungs, clung to his broad shoulders with a tight grip and parted her legs for him. Giving him easier access.

He smiled and the tips of his fangs seemed to wink in the overhead lights. A ripple of something delicious swarmed through her. His fingers moved inside her, his thumb stroking the hard, sensitive bud at her core until her knees trembled and her body screamed for a release it knew was coming.

She rocked on his hand, swiveling her hips, moving into him eagerly, hungrily, all the while caught in the black swirl of his gaze. Again and again, he stroked her inner heat. Again and again, he took her to the very edge of completion, only to stop short and leave her breathless.

"Grayson…"

"Come and let me watch you." His whisper was black silk, smooth and dark, tempting and taunting.

"I need…I need…" She couldn't speak. Could hardly breathe. But oh, she wanted him inside her. Wanted to feel his hard, thick length impale her.

Her body quivered and Tessa gasped. His thumb stroked hard on that bud of sex and she felt the first tiny waves of something fabulous begin to stir. She moved on him, while trying to wiggle out of her jeans so that she could feel more of him. Welcome him higher, deeper.

"Grayson, take me…."

"I am. I will."

She shook her head, licked her lips and watched his eyes spark and flash in reaction to that simple action. "Now, Grayson. Inside me. Now."

He, too, shook his head and then bent to taste her lips, scraping her bottom lip gently with the tips of his fangs. A jolt of something incredible shot through her system like a skyrocket, trailing hot sparks.

"First I will see you go over." He caught her gaze with his as his fingers pressed against her inner walls, coaxing, demanding. "First you will shatter for me."

Standing in her kitchen, half-dressed, driven to the point of near madness, Tessa could only agree. "Take me then," she said, her voice jagged with need.

He smiled again, briefly, knowingly, as if he sensed how close to shattering she really was. Then he pulled his hand free of her, sliding his fingers from her heat until she wanted to weep from the loss of his touch. But before she could complain, he'd pushed her jeans down and off, lifted her off her feet and sat her down naked on the cold, granite countertop.

"Grayson…" She flinched against the feel of the cold counter on her bare skin.

His strong hands parted her thighs, his fingertips stroking her skin in long, feather-soft caresses. She shivered. His gaze locked on hers as he slowly bent down in front of her and heat whipped through her like a lightning strike. He touched her core and she jolted. He smiled, bent his head to her and whispered, "Come for me."

The kitchen lights shone down on his thick, dark hair as he dipped his head to the heart of her. She watched, breathless, as his mouth covered her. The first flick of his tongue sent her on a wildly spinning spiral. She was so ready. So close to implosion it was all she could do to hang on. But she did. She didn't want this to end too quickly. Wanted to feel it all, make it last.

His lips and tongue worked at her most intimate flesh. The tips of his fangs scraped against her and she shivered, caught in a whirl of sensation so thick, so hot, she could hardly draw a breath. She ran her hand through his hair, holding his head to her, watching—unable, unwilling to look away—as he tasted her.

He took her higher than she'd ever gone before. He made her tremble with need, with hunger. He turned her body into a pool of molten desire, until she was mindless with the craving that gripped her in a tight fist.

He suckled her and Tessa splintered. She cried out his name as everything inside her shattered into millions of jagged pieces. She felt as if she were bursting apart in a flash of light that was so blinding she closed her eyes against the magic of it.

And before her body's relentless quaking had ended, Grayson stood, gathered her up close and lifted her off the counter. She wrapped her legs around his middle, and dipped her head to kiss him.

"Free me." Two words, wrenched from his throat.

Tessa saw the control etched onto his features. Lips flat, jaw tight.

"Do it, Tessa." He ground out the words in a brief sentence that was both command and plea.

"Oh, yeah." She reached down between their bodies and unzipped his jeans, reaching into the denim fabric to curl her fingers around his thick erection.

He groaned at her touch and she smiled, knowing he needed as desperately as she did.

Keeping her gaze locked with his, she guided him to her and then slowly slid down on him, taking his hard, full length inside her. Now it was she who groaned. She, whose body stretched to accommodate him, feeling him fill her completely. Feeling the rightness of it all.

What sort of game was Fate playing with them? Bringing them together over Christmas, letting them each find so much in the other, only to have to let each other go again. Why? She wanted. Wanted him to stay. Wanted to be with him always.

As she stared into those dark eyes of his, she knew the truth and wouldn't hide from it, no matter what it cost her.

"I love you."

He stilled. His body locked inside hers, his arms wrapped around her, his mouth only a breath away, he watched her as if she were a miracle to him. And Tessa knew that even if he never said aloud those three words to her…he felt them. He loved her. She felt it. In his touch. In his gaze.

Tomorrow was Christmas Eve and in her heart, she whispered a prayer, silently begging for a kind of Christmas miracle so that she and Grayson could be together. And even though she knew it was hopeless…she couldn't quash the heartfelt wish.

"Tessa—"

"Shh…" She laid her fingers against his mouth and shook her head. "You don't have to say anything. I only wanted you to know how I feel. How I will *always* feel."

Then she moved on him, riding him, up and

down, taking him within, releasing him on a slow glide only to capture him deep again. And the quiet in the room surrounded them. Her heartbeat thundered in the stillness. Her breath set their rhythm.

And this time, when she felt the wash of sensation, he joined her—his body shuddering as he emptied himself into her.

Grayson's great strength trembled. If his heart could have beaten, it would have been clattering in his chest. He held the world in his arms and it was all the more sweet because he knew he wouldn't be able to keep her.

He bent his head to hers and lifted one hand to smooth her hair back from her face. And he knew he would always be able to feel the slide of those short, dark curls across his fingers. He would wake up in years to come, reaching for her. He would find her in his dreams and remember what it was to be loved.

"Tessa," he whispered, "I wish I could give you what you have given me."

"Don't. You don't have to say anything, Grayson."

He paused, looked into her eyes and said only, "You humble me."

She smiled. "That's not my intention."

Carefully, gently, he disengaged their bodies and reluctantly set her on her feet. While she grabbed up her jeans and tugged them on, he adjusted himself, zipped his jeans and tried not to acknowledge the loss of her. It was coming. When this storm ended, when he could get Damon to answer his phone, he would throw his allegiance to the king and Tessa would be safe. Damon's opposition would leave Grayson alone as soon as he'd taken a stand, and once he left, there would be no reason for vampires to come here.

She flipped her hair back out of her eyes and smiled at him again, and Grayson felt an ache where his heart used to be.

It had been a hundred and fifty years since he had been loved. And the last woman who loved him had died a terrifying death. He wouldn't allow that to happen again. He would keep Tessa safe. And then he would ensure that safety by leaving her.

Forever.

The storm eased off a bit during the night and the long, gray day of Christmas Eve. By nightfall, the snow was no more than a few flurries and the wind no longer howled like a banshee.

Yet still, Tessa's nerves were frazzled.

Mainly because Grayson was so obviously on edge. He left the house frequently, never going far, stalking through the snowy woods, hunting for whoever—or whatever—was out there waiting.

But she knew it was more than that. It wasn't only the hunt that drew him into the icy cold. He was trying to pull back from her. Trying to start the separation that was looming closer with every tick of the clock.

Tossing the dishtowel onto the counter, she gave her pasta sauce a quick stir, sending clouds of fragrant steam lifting off the surface of the pot. Then she turned a dial on the stove and a gas flame bloomed under a pot of water. Once that boiled, she'd cook the pasta, then serve dinner and pretend that they were an ordinary couple—though Grayson didn't really eat—for as long as she could.

A knock on the door startled her.

Fear spiked in a heartbeat as she walked from the kitchen into the living room. The scent of pine and cinnamon candles greeted her as she moved slowly across the room. Grayson wouldn't knock on the door and who else would be out in this kind of weather?

Was it her stalker? Finally tiring of moving through the woods frightening her from a distance? Was it a vampire looking for Grayson?

Her hands shook so she clasped them together as she neared the front door. Through the upper glass portion of the door, she saw a middle-aged man standing hunched in his overcoat, with a dark brown hat pulled down over his ears.

Vampires couldn't come in unless they were invited.

"Perfect," she told herself in a harsh whisper.

"Vampire rules you learned in movies. What makes you think they're right?" And why hadn't she asked Grayson?

The man's head lifted as she came to the other side of the door. "Sorry to bother you…"

Instinct made her want to reach for the doorknob and turn it. She fought that instinct and spoke to him through the closed door. "Yes?"

He gave her a tired smile and she noticed small lines of strain etched into the corners of his eyes and beside his mouth. "Don't blame you for not opening up. Very smart. Ladies have to be careful."

"Can I help you?" she asked.

He seemed so tired. So worn out. He lifted one hand to scrub at the dark stubble on his jaw, then he heaved a sigh and looked over his shoulder at the road behind him. "Got turned around in the storm. I'm headed into Whisper for Christmas dinner with my sister." He looked back at her, smiled and shrugged. "But can't figure out quite how to get there from here."

Lost. Well, that was reasonable. Her heartbeat eased back from full throttle. If he were a vampire, he'd have been trying to get her to open the door. And he wasn't Justin, so that was good. Tessa took a deep breath and released it on a sigh. She felt even more relaxed when she spotted Grayson, headed across the yard toward her.

Following her gaze, the man on the porch said, "Ah, this must be your husband. Maybe he can help me."

Tessa opened the door.

Grayson shouted, "No!"

The man grabbed her by the throat.

Chapter 11

Her air was cut off as the vampire held her in a tight grip, dragging her up until she was balanced precariously on the tips of her toes. *Idiot.* She couldn't believe she'd been so stupid. But she'd seen Grayson. Figured she was safe. And the man—vampire—had seemed so harmless. God, she was going to die and all because she had had a moment of sheer stupidity.

"I will snap her neck," the vampire called out in a strong, deep voice. "You know I will, Gray. You move on me and she's dead."

Grayson approached the house with slow, measured steps. He didn't hurry. Didn't threaten.

But through her darkening vision, Tessa saw the fury stamped on his face and the steely determination glinting in his dark eyes. She kept her gaze on him as it faded, because if she were to die, she wanted to go with his face the last thing she saw.

"Let her go, Samuel," Grayson said, his deep voice carrying over the icy wind with a cold far more dangerous than the weather.

"No." The vampire glanced at his captive, then looked back at Grayson. "Not until you swear to support the new king."

Damn…supporters of both sides were after him and Grayson wanted it all over. He'd brought this down on Tessa. Dragged danger to her door and invited death to come calling. Again.

"I've already decided to support Damon, so let her go."

Instantly, the vampire released her and Tessa staggered until she was bracing her back against the doorjamb. Bent in half, she struggled for air, holding the base of her throat as if she could massage a breath into her lungs.

"Tessa? You all right?"

She nodded, looked up at him and *screamed* as a man stepped out of the house and grabbed her from behind.

"Back off!"

"Justin, no!" Tessa squirmed in the man's grasp,

scraping at his hands with her nails, kicking back with her heels as she fought to free herself.

The man who'd stalked her. Who'd driven her with fear for years. This, then, was who had slaughtered that deer. This was the man who'd haunted the woods and eluded Grayson for days. Scenting him now, Grayson found only emptiness in the man's mind and knew why he hadn't been able to track his quarry. Madness had eliminated all rational thought. Justin's mind was a black void.

"Shut up!" Justin shouted, pulled a handgun from his waistband and fired off a shot through the porch roof. Snow scattered in response and Tessa's scream dropped to a low keening. "You back the hell off, both of you! She's mine and she's gonna stay mine or I kill her. Right here. Right now."

Tessa flung one wild look at Grayson and the heart he used to have trembled. He couldn't risk her safety by trying to reason with a madman. In a blink, Grayson moved so quickly, he was nothing more than a blur of motion. He reached the porch, snatched Tessa free of Justin's grasp and shoved her into the house. "Lock the door!"

Panicked, she grabbed at the side of the house and turned back to see Justin, infuriated, fire his gun at Samuel before charging Grayson like a bull, head down, arms swinging. Tessa ran to the end of the porch, lifted an old chair and smashed it hard into the edge of the porch. The chair shattered and she bent to grab up one of the heavy chair rungs.

Grayson couldn't spare her another look. He had to trust that she would stay clear of the fight because he would need every ounce of concentration he had to take care of not only Justin, but also the vampire.

Justin charged and Grayson lunged toward him, ready to fight and kill to protect the woman he loved. The woman he would save as he hadn't saved another so long ago.

His fist smashed into Justin's jaw, sending the man sprawling backward into the waiting arms of Samuel, who was oblivious to the bullet that had slammed into his chest. Baring his lethal fangs, he made a grab for Justin.

"He's mine," Grayson warned.

But the other vampire sneered at him. "He shot me. He dies."

Justin screamed, the sound reverberating through the frozen air, then he seemed to remember his gun and fired it again and again. Bullets tore into Samuel's chest, but the vampire wouldn't be stopped.

Samuel grabbed Justin, gave a mighty wrench and twisted his neck in one violent motion. Justin dropped to the porch, dead before he landed.

"Grayson?" Tessa's voice came from behind him, but Grayson couldn't turn. Didn't dare take his gaze from the vampire, who was now studying him with a measuring eye.

"Stay there." Grayson snapped her an order he hoped to hell she followed. Then to the vampire, he said, "Well, Samuel? Do you leave? Or do you die? Your choice."

Samuel smiled, peeling his lips back from his fangs. He stepped over Justin's body and walked in a semicircle past Grayson, who turned with him, ready. Waiting. Body tensed to defend at all costs.

Samuel flashed a look at Tessa. "Your woman looks tasty, Gray."

"Leave her the hell out of this."

"She's in it already." The vampire scented the air, smiled again and scraped the pad of one thumb across the tip of a fang. "She smells of you, Gray. You've had her. Perhaps I will, too."

"You can try…." Tessa spoke up, quiet. Calm.

The vampire laughed, shifted his gaze to Grayson and tipped his head to one side. "So it's true? You support the king, then?"

"I do."

"Too bad." Samuel smiled again as he moved closer. "Michael and I were sent to change your mind. Seems we failed."

"But you said you were from the king," Tessa countered and Grayson wanted to tell her to keep quiet. To stop reminding the vampire of her presence. But he couldn't spare the attention at the moment.

Another fight was coming. And all that stood between Tessa and an early, ugly death, was *him*. He'd failed to save his family so long ago. Tonight, he wouldn't fail. Tonight, Tessa would live.

Even if he died.

"I lied," Samuel told her, spearing Grayson with his gaze. "We had to know where you stood. Now I know. And frankly, I'm glad it worked out like this. Never liked you, Gray. And I'd just as soon see you dust."

Grayson smiled. "Like she said before, you can try…"

The vampire lunged and Grayson met his attack. The two powerful beings clashed in midair, then tumbled from the porch onto the snow-covered yard. Grayson slammed his fist into Samuel's face, felt the punch of it rocket back through his shoulder.

Samuel countered with a snarl and a hiss, and then sprung up from the ground with a movement so quick the eye couldn't track it. Grayson moved to respond, gathering his strength, his power, to batter his opponent. Punches flew, kicks landed and the two vampires hammered at each other with a fury that sounded like thunder rolling.

Samuel drew a knife and slashed with a vicious upper strike, the blade slicing deep into Grayson's side. Pain blossomed, but he didn't let it stop him. Blood pooled and ran freely and Samuel smiled. "I'll take her. As soon as you're dust, I'll take her and then I'll drain her. Die knowing that."

The reflection of the multicolored Christmas lights shone on the snow in a festive pattern belying the life-and-death struggle in the yard. Tessa watched, heart in her throat. She didn't look at the fallen body of Justin, the man who had made her life a living hell for so long.

She couldn't tear her gaze from the man she loved. The man she would lose no matter the outcome of this fight. She clutched the chair rung in one tight fist, moved down the porch steps into the snow and waited for her chance to defend Grayson.

Blood spattered on the snow in brilliant red streaks and fear caught at her sore throat. Breath struggled in and out of her lungs and Tessa's eyes filled with tears she had no time to shed. Again and again the two vampires crashed into each other and each time it happened, she jolted, terrified that Grayson would fall. Terrified that he would be the one to die in a shower of dust.

Then he kicked the knife from Samuel's hand, sending the blade skittering across the yard to bury itself in a snowdrift. And they were on equal ground again. With a fierce slam of his fist, Grayson sent Samuel sprawling, and in an instant, Grayson turned to her, snatched the chair rung from her hand and plunged it into his opponent's chest.

Samuel howled and disappeared in a blinding flash, nothing left of him but the imprint of his body in the fresh snow.

"Grayson!" Tessa raced forward, catching him as he staggered and dropped to his knees.

She sat down heavily in the snow but didn't feel the cold. She was numb. Body. Heart. Mind. *Soul.*

She smoothed her fingers through his hair, ran her gaze over his bloodied, battered body, then cradled him to her. Bending her head, she kissed his forehead and whispered, "Thank you, thank you, Grayson. Oh, God, you're hurt. You're so hurt."

"No." He shook his head and gave her a smile she knew had to cost him. "I'm fine. I'll *be* fine. Doesn't matter anyway. You're safe now."

But at what cost, she screamed silently. Blood gathered and streamed from the deep wound in his side, bruises gathered on his face and a shallow slice across his chest seeped blood onto his shirt. He'd risked everything for her. He'd put his own survival on the line and hadn't pulled back until the danger was gone. Love filled her and overflowed, spilling in tears from her eyes until her vision blurred.

"I love you, Grayson," she said, her voice soft, clouded with the tears that seemed to have no end to them. "I love you so much."

Lifting one hand, he touched her cheek, then let his hand drop again. "Thank you for that," he said. "You will never know what that means to me. You've given me a gift that will be with me eternally, Tessa. Your love will see me through all the dark years to come."

She bent her head and her tears fell onto his face, and Grayson felt their weight and blessed them. He'd found something here in the place that had held his nightmares for so many years. He'd found peace. And love. And though he had to turn his back on what she offered, the fact of its existence was more than he had ever thought to feel again.

"Come inside," she said, already shifting to help him up.

"No." He shook his head and blinked when snowflakes drifted down to land on his eyelashes. "Never think I don't want to be with you, Tessa. Never think that." His gaze caught hers and Tessa felt the power in that look. The strength. The resolve. The deep regret.

The wind sighed around them, snow dusted their faces, their bodies, encapsulating them in a world of white and cold. "But I have to leave," he said softly. "Now. While I still can. And before another assassin shows up."

"No," she said, her voice breaking on the single word. "Don't go, Grayson. Stay with me."

"You were made for sunlight, Tessa. And I belong in the shadows." Grayson looked at her, etching this moment, this image, in his memory, so that he could draw on it in the empty centuries to come. Backlit by the Christmas lights, by the swirl of snow in the icy wind, she was everything he'd ever wanted. Everything that he could ever need.

And for the first time in more than a century, Grayson wished that he were alive. That he could feel his heart beat. That he could take her hand and walk in the sun. That he could live here, with Tessa. Make children with her. Grow old with her. And though he knew it was futile, he yearned as he had wanted nothing else in his far too long life. Giving her a smile he didn't feel, he said, "You've given me a priceless Christmas gift, Tessa. Because of you, I learned to love again. Because of you, I felt almost alive again. And I will never forget you. Know that. Believe that. And let it be enough."

From inside the house, a clock chimed, counting off the hours between tonight and tomorrow— between Christmas Eve and Christmas morning.

One. Two. Three.

Reaching up, he cupped the back of her head in his palm and drew her down to him. His mouth met hers. She tasted of life, of love, of promise. And for a heartbeat of time, he lost himself in all that she was.

Four. Five. Six.

"I will love you always," Tessa sighed, her tears raining down on his face.

Seven. Eight. Nine.

He pushed himself up, drew her into his arms and held her close.

Ten. Eleven.

The wind died.

The snow sighed to a stop.

The world took a breath and held it.

Twelve.

Grayson gasped, whipped his head back and groaned as pain took root within him and swelled until every fingertip, every cell, every muscle and bone in his body ached and shone with an electrifying agony.

"Grayson?" Tessa's voice. So close. Yet she sounded miles away. "Grayson? Are you all right?"

He hardly heard her over a startling new sound. One he hadn't heard in a century and a half. One he'd never thought to hear again.

His own heart.

Beating.

Grayson drew a breath and then another. He felt his lungs expand. Felt the cold beneath him and the warmth of Tessa's touch on his face. The rhythm of his heartbeat shuddered through him and when he turned to look into Tessa's eyes, he could hardly see her through the sheen of tears clouding his own.

"What is it? Grayson—what?"

Wordlessly, he captured her hand in his and held it to his chest. Her gaze filled with wonder, with amazement, and he shared it with her. Knew that it only meant something because of her. That this miracle had happened to them—for them—because of the strength of what they had found together.

"You're alive?" She grinned, cried a bit more and then threw herself into his arms.

The snow began to fly again. The wind sang around them and the world continued to turn.

Staggering to his feet, Grayson winced at the aches and pains that seemed so much more real to him—now that *he* was real again. But none of it meant anything. Nothing could mar this moment.

And nothing in his life would ever mean so much.

"I love you, Tessa," he said, cupping her face in his palms. "I'm alive again. I can say the words and mean them. I can give you what you need and try to be all that you want. Marry me. Love me and let me love you."

"Oh, Grayson, yes!" She threw her arms around his neck and clung to him as if half-afraid to let him go—in case this Christmas miracle should disappear.

But he knew it wouldn't.

For whatever reason…someone had granted him another chance. A miracle.

And in the blush of a new Christmas morning,

Grayson kissed the woman he would love forever and vowed that he would never waste a moment of the new life he'd found.

* * * * *

Maureen Child will be back in
Silhouette Nocturne with more of her
GUARDIAN *stories.*
But next, look for her new miniseries,
THE KINGS OF CALIFORNIA,
launching in March 2008
from Silhouette Desire.

FATE CALLS

CARIDAD PIÑEIRO

To my sister, Carmen, for all her support
and our discussions about the Pagan backgrounds
of some of our traditional Christmas celebrations.

Chapter 1

Death and destruction were the only Christmas gifts that Fate had ever brought Hadrian Aurelius.

Now Fate had delivered him yet one more Christmas calamity—a group of bell-ringing do-gooders who had set up camp across the way from his brownstone, disturbing his daytime slumber and a good chunk of his nights.

The *clang-clang-clang* of the bell would begin midmorning, slipping into his brain as he rested after a long night of prowling the Manhattan streets. Low and sporadic, he could drive the noise out of his head for most of the day, until dusk came and with it, the ringing rose, insistent. Demanding.

Followed too often by a cheery greeting laced with enough sweetness to curdle the meal his keeper brought him at rising.

For weeks Hadrian had told himself he could outlast them. After all, he was a vampire elder and had survived nearly two thousand years of even greater challenges.

But there was just something about that damned bell.

Hadrian jerked off the bedcovers, strode to the window and glanced at the Santa suit-wearing tormentor standing in front of the public library. There was little to discover about the Santa as he stood next to a collection kettle, arm merrily shifting up and down, calling to the passersby to leave a small donation for the homeless.

The soft rasp of knuckles came at his bedroom door—his keeper, George, bringing a snack to help drive away the lethargy of his daytime respite.

"Come in," Hadrian called out, but as George wheeled in the cart bearing the gold chalice filled with warmed blood, Hadrian waved him off.

"Thank you, George, but you may take it away."

He smiled as he peered down at the Santa again. "I think I may be dining out tonight."

The itchy polyester beard chafed her skin. The rough fabric of the suit, a cloth of indeterminate nature, rubbed at a variety of spots, creating discomfort at assorted locations. She wouldn't think about the rank smell that she hadn't been able to get rid of despite careful laundering.

Connie Morales fidgeted—again—with the costume that swam on her petite body, defying the "one size fits all" claims of the manufacturer. With a shrug, she shifted the lopsided shoulders of the suit in an attempt to make it sit better. She ignored the lingering odor and rang her bell, forcing a merry tone to her voice as she called out to the smartly dressed businesswoman walking toward her.

Connie flashed her best smile, uncertain it would be visible beneath the cumbersome beard. Satisfaction came as the lady returned the smile and dropped some change into the collection kettle.

"Thank you for helping the homeless," Connie chimed with false cheer, her words in tune with the rise and fall of her arm and the crisp bright tones of the bell ringing in the chill of the winter air.

Each clang of the coins into the collection kettle brought Connie satisfaction. The silent slip of a bill into the pot was even more rewarding. Each donation meant more for the downtown shelter her upscale, midtown law firm had adopted this holiday season.

As an up-and-coming associate, her decision to

participate in the head partner's pet Christmas project had a number of motivations. Self-interest being the primary one, since the time spent at the shelter and a nice sum in the collection pot would earn her major brownie points with the head man.

Points that might push her toward the partnership she had been working hard to achieve for the last four years. But she had to acknowledge that mixed in with that self-interest was something else that had been awakened within her, forcing her to consider that what she was doing was important to a lot of people who had far less than she did.

The holiday spirit maybe? Connie put renewed fervor into her smile and the swing of her arm.

Her current situation reignited memories of her own Christmases past. The simple gifts beneath the tree, made special by the love with which they were given. Dinners around a table laden with food and blessed with an assortment of her siblings, their children and her parents.

It had been too long since she had allowed that spirit into her holiday season.

Just one more day and her Christmas vacation would start. She would do her best to enjoy this holiday season. In the morning she would start her shopping and prepare herself for a visit to her family.

"Merry Christmas to you as well," she said with a nod and a broad smile at one man who slipped a five-dollar bill into her pot. As she tracked the passage of the alms giver, she noted a well-dressed man step out of the brownstone across the way.

It would have been impossible not to notice him.

Tall. Lean. A fine-boned face that might have been handsome if there had been any hint of life there.

But there was none.

The chiseled lines of his features were harsh. Unyielding. Fashionably tousled shoulder-length dark brown hair framed that austere face. His lips were drawn into a thin slash. She imagined that if he might smile…

Only he didn't.

Instead he shot her a glare that sent a shiver down her spine. He trained dark, almost soulless, eyes on her.

He was the kind of man you didn't want to piss off. His gaze drifted to the bell in her hand, and it occurred to her that it angered him. She had somehow run afoul of him.

Such scrutiny or disdain didn't bother her, however.

She was a lawyer, after all.

Pasting a determined smile on her face, she raised her hand higher and brought the bell down forcefully.

It rang with a resounding peal in the winter night, letting the handsome stranger know that he would not dissuade her from her mission.

* * *

Hadrian fisted his hands at his sides, resisting the urge to throttle the obstinate Santa who defiantly rang the bell as if Hadrian hadn't just shot him an irate glare.

With the power his long vampire age provided him, it wouldn't be difficult to take care of the Santa. In fact, he could do it from here and no one would be the wiser.

But as the Santa imbued his ringing with a more fervent sweep of his arm, Hadrian realized that satisfaction required a more personal approach.

Later, he thought, ripping his gaze from the slight frame of the Santa. It was the first night of Saturnalia and he intended to spend it the way he had when he had been a young man.

When he had been alive.

A night of merriment and other carnal pleasures would be just the thing to drive away the annoyance created by the bell-ringing Santa. Maybe, if he enjoyed himself sufficiently during his revelry, he'd forego ripping out the throat of his red-suited tormentor.

And if he didn't?

A midnight snack always helped put him in a better mood.

Chapter 2

Hadrian sipped at his glass of wine, eyeing the nubile young women parading through the Puck Building, courtesy of his old friend Maximillian.

As one of the city's hottest fashion designers, Maximillian always had the choicest young men and women—along with some of the most powerful vampires in town—at all his affairs.

Tonight was no different.

Tall, lean women bypassed the table laden with food and sashayed to the bar, where they were joined by equally tall and lean men, eager for an opportunity with one of the women or with each other.

Hadrian usually avoided both of those types.

Their blood was weak from their constant fasting and he got no satisfaction from a sexual encounter with a bag of bones.

Not that he got much satisfaction from any sexual encounters lately, he thought, eyeing the crowd and looking for the hangers-on to the Beautiful People. The stylists, PR people and others were closer to his tastes and easy to charm into a quick tryst.

He spied one attractive young woman by the buffet table, loading up a plate with delicacies. She was of average height, with doe-brown eyes and a bob of chocolate brown hair that framed a pleasant face.

Her body was also pleasant, Hadrian thought. Full breasts—real, if he were any judge—with an average waist and boyish hips. While he liked his women more rounded, there was something pleasing about this young lady's overall appearance.

"Pleasing" being the most emotion a woman could rouse in him after his long existence filled with countless unnamed partners.

After nearly two thousand years, there was nothing that brought satisfaction anymore. And in those moments after, when he put his fangs to a woman's throat and fed, anger rose sharply, obliterating all other emotions, dampening the fulfillment of all other demands.

Anger that a vampire had turned him.

Anger that the humans had destroyed the life he had made for himself after being sired.

Hadrian drew in a sharp breath, controlling the fury that surged through him as he took note of the humans and vampires unwittingly milling together in the crowd. The humans had no awareness of the immortals circulating amongst them while the demons were sizing up the mortals the way a diner might pick a lobster out of a tank.

He didn't rightly know who he hated more.

The largest part of the crowd was gathered in the grand ballroom of the Puck Building, where Maximillian had decided to hold his "little" gathering to celebrate the holiday season and a recent launch of a line specially designed for one of the country's leading department stores.

Close to five hundred people circulated inside the ballroom and adjacent gallery. A long line of party-goers waited outside in the cold, eager to be part of tonight's festivities.

"Stop glowering so," Maximillian said as he approached and draped an arm around Hadrian's shoulders.

He shot a glance out of the corner of his eye at his flamboyant friend. Disregarding the no-white-after-Labor-Day rule, Maximillian was in a loose-fitting white tunic embroidered with ornate golden lace along the sleeves, hem and neckline. Equally loose-fitting white pants flowed beneath the tunic.

It reminded Hadrian of the togas the two had worn in their youth—before a Saturnalian tryst with a newfound love had ended both their lives.

Hadrian gestured to the decorations. "Did you choose all this as a lark?"

"Do you not find it festive?" Maximillian replied with a flippant wave of his hand and a girlish trill in his voice.

Boughs of greenery and wreaths adorned the various walls and arches. Golden suns and stars decorated the boughs of pine and holly. Scattered here and there were small pine trees, also laden with golden ornaments and trimmed with rich purple ribbons. The aroma of fresh evergreens and the decorations brought a memory of his holidays back in Rome. With that memory came intense pain.

"I find it torturous."

Maximillian leaned close, as a lover might, and whispered in his ear, "Maybe because you are unable to forgive and enjoy, *mio amico.*"

Before Hadrian could reply, Maximillian flounced to the bar, where a young man and woman appeared to be waiting for him. As Maximillian placed an arm around each of their waists, he shot a wink and a broad smile at Hadrian as if in invitation.

Maybe Maximillian can find callow joy in their

arms, but I cannot, Hadrian thought, declining the invitation with a slight bow of his head.

A waiter paused before him and he snagged a glass of red wine from the serving tray. Another server drifted close, offering an assortment of appetizers, some gilded in gold as was the Roman custom. Hadrian waved for the man to leave and peered through the crowd for the woman he had spotted earlier, intending to introduce himself and seduce her into a quiet nook where he could sate his hunger.

He slowly walked through the crowd, battling the scents and noises that grated on his heightened vampire senses. A band played loudly from one corner, forcing an escalation in the volume of those attempting to converse.

As he passed through the crowd, more than one woman attempted to snare his attention with a welcoming look, but he was immune to such entreaties. Only if he failed with his intended target would he settle for someone else. In retrospect, the chase had become the only fun part of the game for him since the end of the hunt usually brought so little fulfillment.

He continued onward and finally found her, looking forlorn and slightly out-of-place in a far corner of the adjacent room. She held a half-empty glass of wine in her hand. As he approached and flashed her a smile, the hand holding the glass wavered.

It was not as noisy in the corner she had chosen, but still he sat beside her on the ledge of the window and leaned close. "It's nice to find a quiet spot, isn't it?"

"I'm supposed to be meeting people, but this is my first big event. It's a little overwhelming." She shot him a shy smile and brought her glass up for a shaky sip.

"Maximillian is known for overdoing it." He drank from his own glass before stammering, "So sorry. I'm Hadrian and you are…?"

"Patricia. Do you know Maximillian personally?" An awed tone flavored her question.

"We've been friends for a very long time, but these gatherings can be…tiresome. Would you like to go somewhere quieter? Maybe get a bite to eat?"

Her hand trembled again before she faced him and examined him carefully, clearly attempting to first determine if he were serious, and then if he were trustworthy. Her priorities were reversed, much as his had been so long ago.

Maybe if he'd had his priorities straight, his life would have turned out differently.

He must have passed muster since she asked, "Where would you like to go?"

Humans were sometimes too easy, Hadrian thought as he slipped his arm through hers and led her from the building.

* * *

Connie's arm ached from the many swings of the bell. As she surreptitiously glanced at her watch, she realized it was late, time to go home, especially since the residential street had become nearly deserted.

They had chosen the spot in front of the library in a tony East Side neighborhood both for safety's sake and because of the possibility of increased profit. Despite the relative safety of the area, she knew staying anywhere too late could prove risky. Besides, the library had closed nearly an hour earlier and foot traffic was virtually gone, minimizing the possibility of donations.

She grabbed the collection kettle, intending to put it in the small office to which the library had so generously given them access. As she did so she caught a glimpse of a man across the way. He was hidden in the shadows cast by the stoop of the brownstone.

For a moment she wondered if it was the handsome man she had seen earlier, but he remained in the shadows, making her uneasy. With the key the librarian had provided, she opened the door, slipped inside and locked it behind her. Moving quickly, she safely stored that night's donations and the kettle. Removing her purse from the drawer of a nearby desk, she walked back to the main glass doors of the library.

Still slightly unnerved by the man in the shadows, she scanned the street for any sign of him. It appeared clear. As a police car paused just past the door of the library, she left, heading toward Lexington Avenue and the subway line that would take her home to her small studio in Chelsea.

As she walked, she occasionally shot a glance over her shoulder, searching, but everything appeared to be in order and she wrote off the man in the shadows to her imagination. Maybe she had been wishfully thinking about getting another look at the handsome devil who had stepped out of the luxurious brownstone earlier that night.

Get ahold of yourself, Connie. Anyone who looks like him and lives in this pricey area is well out of my league. She was definitely one for pretzels and beer, not caviar and champagne. The thought brought a rumble to her stomach, reminding her that she hadn't had a chance to grab a bite to eat before beginning her Santa shift.

Her mouth salivated as she passed a Chipotle restaurant. Although she was Cuban, she could eat Mexican food every day of the week, but with the winter chill, her favorite burrito bowl would be ice cold by the time she got home. Not to mention that she was trying to lose a few pounds to make up for those she would surely gain thanks to all the upcoming holiday meals and festivities.

Her hips were already too rounded to withstand that extra weight.

It will be a diet TV dinner for me, Connie thought as she swiped her way through the subway turnstile and hurried down to the platform. A few other passengers waited there, students at nearby Hunter College, judging from the looks of them.

With a slow-building rush of air from the tunnel and a rumble beneath her feet, the subway announced its imminent arrival. The loud squeal and hiss of brakes grated against her ears before the train came to a stop in the station.

She boarded and was soon on her way to Union Square. The area had become upscale several years back, although Connie's studio was a few blocks over on Fourteenth Street and in a part of town that wasn't necessarily so upscale. Yet. Gentrification was quickly moving her way.

The small studio suited her just fine. It was a good investment until she could make partner and maybe find someone and settle down with a house and children in the suburbs. A predictable life, but then again, such predictability matched her nature.

She had always been the go-to girl. The one everyone counted on to be stable and responsible. Others might find that boring, but she found it reassuring.

It took barely fifteen minutes to reach her stop

and another ten before she was slipping the key into the lock for her studio condo.

As she opened the door, a familiar meow greeted her.

Her black cat Osiris eagerly waited inside. When she entered, the cat meowed once again and proceeded to twine sinuously around her legs in welcome.

Connie bent, scooped up the cat and hugged her tight, earning a growling protest. She released the animal, who followed her into the kitchen.

Osiris's gaily decorated ceramic food bowl sat empty. The automatic water fountain sputtered angrily from a lack of water. Clearly these were the reasons for the vocal welcome.

Connie filled the two bowls first before popping her frozen dinner into the microwave and changing into her warm, comfortable sweats.

Then she pulled out the sofa bed in the living area and turned on the television. The late night news was on, but she flipped through the stations until she located reruns of one of her favorite law enforcement dramas.

Something about the eternal good-versus-evil fight always intrigued her. It was why she had become a lawyer. Although a year in the district attorney's office had shown her how misguided her decision had been. After plea bargaining more cases than she wished to think about, she had opted to continue her career in a law firm where at least she knew what kinds of people she was representing.

The microwave beeped, pulling her from her thoughts.

As she did every night that she wasn't working late on a case or meeting colleagues for a drink, Connie grabbed her dinner and slipped beneath the sheets of her bed. As she ate, her mind was half on the television drama and half on the man she had seen earlier.

Scooping up a bit of the low-fat—translation: low-taste—macaroni and cheese, she wondered why he had stayed on her mind for so long. She wasn't one to let a pretty face sway her. She was too sensible for that.

Maybe it was the anger in the dark, glaring gaze he had turned her way. Anger and maybe even pain.

Melodramatic much? she kidded herself. Despite her generally sensible nature, she had always been a bit of a dreamer, devouring countless romance novels and romantic movies. Yes, she thought, there was a soft side to the tough cookie lawyer she presented to the rest of the world.

The tough cookie lawyer who spent way too many hours at the office, preventing much of a social life.

If Connie was honest with herself, that was the real reason for her fascination with the unknown stranger—she'd had no one besides her cat to warm her sheets in quite a long time.

The cat jumped up on the bed and settled herself at Connie's feet, padding the space with her paws and circling around until she was comfortable enough to bed down. A contented purr soon vibrated up Connie's legs and warmth built slowly at her feet.

A sad and inadequate replacement for the hard heat of a man's body.

Connie finished the TV dinner and sank against the pillows, careful not to dislodge the cat and double checking to make sure her alarm was set. If she saw the handsome man tomorrow, she might just do something about changing her current situation.

Chapter 3

Her warmth surrounded him, slick and welcoming, as Hadrian pumped into her, rousing her passion.

She moaned and clutched at his shoulders. Dug her nails deep and raised her hips to bury him within her. Her soft cries spurred him on, but he knew that when her release came, there would be only one thing he would want.

Only one thing that would bring him some small measure of satisfaction.

He watched her intently. A fine flush had spread across her ample breasts, which bobbed gently from the force of his thrusts. Her light caramel-colored nipples were beaded into tight points from the earlier caress of his mouth. He could still see the slight dampness of his kiss.

Bending his head, he sucked her nipple into his mouth once again and she mewled her pleasure at the strong tug. She fisted her hands into his hair to urge him on.

He felt it then, building inside of him. The lust of the demon. Human lust had long eluded him. The man within had been dead for far too long.

Around his erection, the throb and tightening of her body told him she was almost there, almost ready for him to take his final pleasure.

He intensified the motion of his hips, dragging a gasp from her that was part pleasure, part pain. He didn't like the pain, but life had taught him that the two were irrevocably intertwined.

He jabbed into her again and it began. He heard it in the way her heart skipped a beat and her blood rushed through her body, bringing her release. She screamed her pleasure, her head thrown back against the pillows, her heels digging into the mattress to increase his penetration.

It was time.

As he continued to pump his hips, drawing out her climax, he nuzzled the neck she had bared to him. He could smell the muskiness of her arousal. Beneath his lips he felt the wild rush of blood, singing through her veins.

Dragging his fangs from his mouth, he brushed those fangs along her fragile skin and she stiffened, aware that something wasn't quite right.

It would be the last thing she would remember in the morning, he thought, sinking his fangs deep into her neck and feeding from the passion-laced blood surging through her body.

She cried out in pain, but as the vampire's kiss swept over her, the cry became a long moan of pleasure. The human responded to the demon's call and she held his head to her neck and begged for more.

It was only then, with her blood beginning a wild ride through his system, energizing him with life, that he could experience pleasure.

Time and time again Hadrian plunged into her as he fed. Soon, he knew he had to stop. If he fed even one more drop, she would not survive. Ripping himself from her neck, he thrust into her one last time and released his seed.

Dead seed unless he turned her. Only then, with the sire's kiss running through her veins, could that seed bestow life within. Only then, and only if she was at the peak of her fertility.

Tonight, she was just another empty vessel, pleasuring the demon with her blood while the man trapped within remained dead.

This was the way of his life now. Cold. Empty. Barren.

As he left the body of the woman, now growing limp beneath him from loss of blood, anger surged through him.

For some inexplicable reason, the anger brought the remembrance of the Santa, cheerily ringing in the holiday. He imagined how he might silence that Santa and smiled.

Bah, humbug.

The weather had taken a drastic drop into the low twenties, and with the wind chill, the temperature hovered in the single digits. By nighttime, there was a threat the temperature might even drop below zero.

But the weather hadn't stopped Connie from accepting her turn at the collection kettle. She had prepared herself that morning with a visit to a local sporting goods store, where in addition to the purchase of some Mets jerseys and T-shirts for her brother-in-law and nephews, she had grabbed some space-age undergarments that promised to ward off even a subzero chill.

It helped that the collection kettle was positioned in the sun. The weak winter rays had created a nice bit of warmth when she had initially taken over the station. Likewise, the large building on the corner stopped the worst of the wind. Keeping in constant motion helped the most, however. She marched back and forth on the sidewalk and kept her arm in constant motion, ringing the bell, summoning the pedestrians who braved the cold and occasionally offered up a donation.

When one arm grew tired, she switched the bell to the other. The passersby seemed to understand the strength of her determination on such a wicked winter day. The greater part of the contributions had been dollar bills, providing her with incentive to keep on with her task despite the growing numbness of her fingers and the sting of the wind on her cheeks.

Night fell more quickly that day. Or maybe it only felt that way since as soon as the last of the sun's rays disappeared, the cold bit deep through the Santa suit and her thermal underwear. She quickened her pace along the sidewalk, hoping the increased speed would warm her. The bell rang in time with her footfalls.

One step, two steps, ring the bell. She tried to keep a rhythm and bring warmth to her increasingly cold extremities.

One step, two steps…

"Stop that."

Connie had been concentrating so hard that she hadn't registered the approach of the man.

The first thing she noticed was his expensive black shoes blocking her path. She moved her gaze upward past stylish charcoal-gray slacks and a camel-colored cashmere overcoat.

A scarf with an unexpectedly wild pattern—Maximillian's signature colors and design—led to a strong chin and full lips constricted in a grimace of displeasure.

The handsome man from the day before.

He had slipped into her dreams more than once last night. Erotic dreams filled with naughty imaginings of what they might do within the walls of his luxury town house. Definitely sexier than her studio sofa bed.

Moving her gaze up the final few inches, it connected with the dark intimidating features she had recalled. Annoyance was still stamped on his masculine face.

"Excuse me?" she asked, slightly irritated by his command and the way in which he'd stepped into her path, invading her personal space. He stood barely inches from her, his presence unusually dominating.

"Can you please stop that infernal ringing?" At his sides, his hands fisted open and closed.

"It's part of the job, the bell-ringing." She motioned to the collection kettle sitting unattended just a few feet away.

"I think the Santa suit and pot are enough of a clue as to what you want. There's no need for the bell."

"We have a permit—"

"I don't care what you have. How much will it take to silence that damn ringing?" Hadrian asked, his voice escalating with anger at each word. Surely the Santa standing before him had a price for his silence. Everyone had a price after all.

The Santa eyed him up and down, as if taking his measure. Then the Santa met his gaze with determined blue-gray eyes framed by exceptionally long, thick lashes. "It wouldn't be right…"

The wind whipped up as the Santa spoke, displacing the beard and muffling the last of the response. With annoyance, he said, "Can you take off that hideous masquerade so we can speak like civilized individuals?"

As the Santa whipped off the hat and beard, Hadrian realized what a major mistake he had made. Beneath the costume was a woman. A rather beautiful one at that, stunning him into momentary silence.

He should have realized it was a female beneath the costume from her slight build and the higher pitch of her voice.

She raised her face to peer up at him. She was several inches shorter than his over six-foot height.

That blue-gray gaze settled on his face, cheeks pale from the chill. Lusciously pouty lips slicked with some kind of gloss tightened with disapproval. With careful precision, as if she were speaking to a child, she repeated her earlier statement, "It would be wrong to take a donation to stop ringing the bell."

"It would be wrong because—"

"You should give freely from your heart. Not because you want something in exchange," she said and inched up her chin a determined notch.

"Because the holiday spirit is all about giving," he replied, his tone saying otherwise, although the determined young woman before him didn't react to his sarcasm.

She narrowed her gaze, creating a deep furrow between perfectly waxed brows. "Are you a Scrooge?"

A Scrooge. He'd been called worse things in his long existence and by people far more powerful than the little chit standing before him. If earthly incentives wouldn't help silence the bell, there were other ways. Vampire ways. He was an elder, after all.

"You will not ring the bell again tonight." He raised his hand as if to stay hers and called forth a smidgen of his immortal's power to control her.

To his surprise, the young woman battled him, slowly raising her hand even as he increased the force of his vampire thrall.

"What are you doing?" she asked, every muscle in her body straining to defy him.

"You will not ring the bell," he repeated, but even as he did so, he sensed the purpose of her will, pushing back at him. Amazing him. There were few vamps who could fight the thrall of an elder and here she was…

A young, vital and desirable woman showing him more spirit than he had experienced in a long time.

Maybe ever.

Raising both hands, he reached deep inside himself and summoned more of his power. He focused it on her and the bell in her hand, and sent his command to her telepathically.

Put the bell down and come with me.

Surprise slammed into his body as she mentally replied, *I don't want to.*

Redoubling his efforts, he repeated his command. This time she slowly bent at the knees and placed the bell on the ground. As he walked across the street, she followed, but in his brain he heard her complaint.

You can't control me forever.

With a laugh, as they ascended the steps to his brownstone, he said, *We'll see.*

Chapter 4

Once inside, he shut the door behind them with a sweep of his hand and faced her.

With the brisk winter wind gone, a slightly sour aroma permeated the air around her. He wrinkled his nose and motioned to the Santa suit.

"Take it off."

Her hands clenched into tight fists at her sides and once again, he felt the pull and push of power between them as she defied him.

Interesting.

He took a step closer and raised his hand to the neck of the Santa suit, where he found the pull for the zipper. As the back of his hand skimmed the slick black shirt beneath, her body trembled.

"Don't tell me you're a virgin," he said while slowly drawing down the zipper on the suit, revealing the ample curves of her breasts beneath the shimmer of the tight-fitting fabric.

He suddenly itched to touch those breasts, but contained himself.

Before pleasure came punishment for her defiance.

To his continued surprise, she tilted back her head and with only a slight hitch in her voice to give away her discomfort said, "Just because I'm not a virgin doesn't mean I'm not virtuous. I dislike being pawed by the likes of you."

Hadrian chuckled as he completely unzipped the top of the Santa suit. "The likes of me?"

"You won't get away with this."

He laughed again, amused by her spirit. "Who will stop me?"

He picked up his hand and once again had to fight the urge to cup her breast. His human desire confused him. It had been quite some time since he had felt it. Instead of giving in to it, he cradled the side of her face and leaned close until his nose barely brushed hers.

"Who will stop me? You?"

"Yes, me." Her voice exploded against his lips, the spill of her breath warm and all too tempting.

A harsh laugh escaped him this time as he met her gaze. "How will you—"

"There are laws—"

"And I suppose you know all those laws," he said and inched his hand downward, but not to her breast. Instead, he slipped his hand beneath the fabric at her shoulder. With a forceful nudge he sent the offensive Santa suit to the parquet floor.

"I'm a lawyer," she said, reaching for his hands as he moved to the drawstring at her waist.

His laugh this time was sharp and unrestrained. "A lawyer. There are some who might say there is not much difference between the two of us."

Her eyebrows narrowed once again before she thoughtfully asked, "And why is that?"

He unleashed the demon, transforming into a vampire. When he spoke, his voice was tinged with the low rumble of the beast he had let loose.

"Because we are both bloodsuckers, aren't we?"

The blood drained from Connie's body, creating the chill of fear as she examined the demon who now stood before her.

The dark chocolate-brown of his pupils had bled out, replaced by an eerie neon blue-green glow. Long and lethal-looking fangs had erupted from beneath the edge of his full top lip, past his pouty lower lip, down to the middle of his chin.

She had placed her hands over his as they rested

at the tie to the suit's drawstring. Now she knew that the cold of his skin wasn't from the weather outside.

And then she told herself she had to be dreaming or hallucinating. There were no such things as vampires. Closing her eyes, she willed herself to wake, but when she opened her eyes again, things were as they had been before. This was all too real.

Containing her fear and summoning every last bit of her courage, she said, "Then I guess you owe me some professional courtesy."

The hands resting beneath hers jumped. He shifted back to peruse her face. Arching a lush, dark brow, he asked, "Professional courtesy?"

"From one bloodsucker to another."

The laughter that erupted from him was full and rich as he threw his head back. His body shook with it.

Human mirth, she thought, since it lacked the earlier animal rumble she had heard. When he faced her once again, her perception was confirmed. All traces of the vampire were gone and what remained were the handsome features that had snared her attention earlier.

"You are…intriguing."

"Let me go," she said again even as she felt the shove of power that had compelled her to put down the bell and follow him, no matter how hard she tried to fight it.

"I think not."

Beneath her hands, his nimble fingers worked the drawstring and loosened the waistband until the pants puddled at her feet, leaving her standing before him in the tight and rather revealing underwear.

Interest flared in his gaze as he perused her body. To her surprise, she felt herself responding.

He might be a demon, but he was a damned attractive one and he was gazing at her as if he wanted to eat her.

But then again that was what he might truly want to do, Connie reminded herself.

But not before some pleasure, her brain surmised, rocking her with the reality that the man standing before her could control her every thought and action.

Fear came again as it had before. Her body trembled as he moved his hand to her neck, but all he did was pluck the lanyard with the key to the library from around her neck.

He held it out to the side and said, "George."

A man scurried from the shadows behind him. Connie hadn't noticed him standing there before.

"Yes, Hadrian," he said with an obsequious bob of his head.

Hadrian. At least the demon now had a name. An interesting one at that.

Hadrian jiggled the lanyard up and down. "Please take this key and put Miss…"

He paused, waiting for her to answer.

"Connie Morales. And it's *Ms.* Morales."

A glimmer of a smile flashed across his lips before he said, "Please put Ms. Morales's things away, would you? And do something about that Santa suit."

"It is rather rank, isn't it?" George quickly took the key, but had to wait for her to step from the puddle of the pants before he scurried away to do Hadrian's bidding.

"Do you always get what you want?" she asked, intrigued despite the danger of the situation.

In a millisecond the human disappeared and the vampire emerged, his movements so swift they were a blur. And then she felt the sharp edges of his fangs at her neck.

"Always," he said and then pain swept her away as he sank his teeth deep into her flesh.

Full night was upon the city, calling to Hadrian to come out and play. To savor the delights found in the dark, only…

Hadrian looked away from the window and to the woman he had lashed to his bedposts. Her arms were spread wide and her head hung downward as her body rested against some pillows and the ornately carved wood of his headboard. Her ass, plump and deliciously smooth beneath his hands as he had carried her up to his room, pressed onto the mattress.

Maybe he had made her too comfortable, he thought. Maybe a little more punishment would soothe the too smart tongue that had surprised him the night before.

Or maybe it was a bit of professional courtesy, he thought with a smile, recalling her words.

He couldn't see her face since the downward position of her head had brought her chestnut-colored shoulder-length hair cascading forward to hide the bulk of her features. A bit of the straight slash of her patrician nose peeked out from the wealth of hair, along with a hint of her full lips, glossy still from whatever women applied to their lips these days.

But what he couldn't see rose up in his memory. Blue-gray eyes that revealed a sharp wit. High cheekbones pink with the flush of life. Her mouth again, full and mobile as she dared to defy him.

He imagined silencing that mouth with his lips and need slammed through him, awakening desire. Bringing forth a human arousal such as he had not experienced in quite some time.

Taking a deep breath, he clenched his hands at his sides and wondered what she had awakened within him. Wondered how he would satisfy that need without losing a bit of himself. Despite all that he had done in the many years of his existence, he still considered himself a man of morals.

So why did you kidnap her? his inner voice demanded.

The truth of it was, he didn't know why.

In his many millennia of undead life, he had never taken a woman without asking—sexually or otherwise. The feeding he did afterward—he considered it payback for the pleasure he brought his conquests.

Taking someone in anger or to control them was generally not his thing.

So what do you plan to do with her now? his inner voice—his rusty conscience, he realized—asked with more purpose.

But before he had a chance to consider it further, he noticed the slight movement of her head. It sank forward for a second before jerking backward, the movement sending the spill of her dark hair shifting with the motion.

She groaned and shook her head as the daze from his feeding fled her body.

He walked to the edge of the bed and anxiously awaited the moment when full consciousness returned to her. Preparing himself for when she saw him once again. For her reaction.

What would it be like to see pleasure slip into her gaze?

Her head shifted from side to side before she sensed him and looked his way. Her blue-gray eyes—slate blue he decided—were unfocused at first, but they soon honed in on him. Then her gaze skittered to either of her wrists.

She tugged at them, but he had done a fine job of securing her with the soft bindings he had fashioned from one of his silk robes.

"Is this what you plan to do? Keep me around as a private buffet?"

As she had last night, she dragged a smile to his face with her daring. He decided in that instant that what he wanted to do more than anything else was to see just how far that daring would last her.

Sauntering to the bed, he sat on its edge and cupped her cheek. "A buffet? You don't strike me as being so pedestrian."

Connie scanned the large bedroom, appointed with luxurious furniture and sensually rich fabrics. Far from her pedestrian and simple tastes. Clearly designed for decadent pleasures, which made her muse, "So if I'm not dinner…"

A small smile came to his lips and, as she had thought the day before, his smile was devastating. Of course, thinking that had her wondering if she was either crazy or under some kind of vampire thrall, considering he had her tied to his bedposts and had already made her a meal.

"Am I dessert? Is that what you do with your visitors?"

The smile evaporated faster than dew in the

morning and he pulled his hand away. "I don't have many visitors."

Connie recalled something from a class she had taken years earlier—establish a connection with your captor. Make him see you as a person rather than an object.

"So you do a lot of take-out I guess," she said, hoping humor would reach whatever humanity remained in him.

One side of his mouth quirked upward. "We seem to be employing a lot of euphemisms for my needs."

"Your needs? You mean bloodsucking, right?"

He cradled her cheek again and asked, "Do you think that's the only thing I need?"

"You're a vampire, right?" she asked, though she was still struggling with the fact that vampires were real.

In response, he traced the outline of her lips with his thumb and as he did so, heat spread from that point outward, awakening her body. As the heat washed over her, her nipples tightened in anticipation and then need slammed into her center, yanking a rough gasp from her.

Her nether lips swelled, heavy with want. Inside her an emptiness arose, begging for fulfillment.

She sucked in a shaky breath as he said, "Man does not live by bread alone."

Her need was so strong it was nearly painful. She

clenched her thighs tight, fighting the demand.
Fighting him, she realized as she met his dark gaze.

"Is this what you give to all your conquests?"

"I give them satisfaction."

The tones of his voice were pitched low, stirring to
life the pleasure points in her body. They were vibrat-
ing with desire as he said, "I can give you fulfillment."

Her breath rasped raggedly in her chest, rough
with want. Between her legs she was drenched, all
her parts swollen and demanding a touch. A stroke
to release the painful tension.

Just ask me to touch you.

"No." She yanked at the bindings and writhed
against the bed, but that accomplished nothing.

Make him realize you are not just an object, she
reminded herself. "Why are you doing this, Hadrian?
I haven't done anything to you."

He abruptly rose from her side, paced back and
forth for a few angry strides before he stalked
back to the edge of the bed. "Why? Does there
have to be a why?"

Even as she battled the passion twisting her body
into knots, Connie realized that this was a question
he'd asked himself countless times. If she was going
to become Hadrian's meal ticket, she wanted to hear
his answer to that question.

"There has to be a why for the way you are,
Hadrian."

Chapter 5

December, 307 A.D.
Rome

Hadrian examined with pride the hundreds of amphora filled with rich wines and oils. He had finished his accounting just minutes earlier and shortly the loaded barge would be going down the Tiber to Ostia to await transport to Carthage.

Life was good, he thought, handing the paperwork for the shipment to his slave, who would accompany the load downriver and then return once it was safely onboard the larger galley to Carthage. Hadrian had already made arrangements with a dealer there to sell his goods and then send the galley back loaded with cotton and papyrus from Egypt.

His man jumped onto the barge. It pulled away from Aventine Hill and the *Forum Vinarium* as dusk fell, spreading brilliant fingers of crimson and indigo through the sky.

Hadrian smiled, pleased with all that he had accomplished that day. Business had been thriving, cementing his position among the *equestrian* class. Glancing down at the gold ring that identified his status to those he met, pride filled him once again.

Pride and anticipation. Now that he had established himself, he could finally approach Alexandra's father and ask for her hand. But before he did...

It was the first night of Saturnalia. He intended to savor the fruits of his success before binding himself to his beloved. His childhood friend, Maximillian, was waiting for him by the Temple of Saturn so they could join the festivities marking the beginning of the celebration of the Winter Solstice.

Maximillian had supposedly arranged for some splendid entertainment for later that night and as Hadrian walked from Aventine Hill toward the temple, he hoped that his friend had restrained his proclivity for the unusual.

He moved quickly toward the temple, caught up in the excitement of the many Romans who filled the streets, also on their way to begin festivities. The homes along the way had been decorated for the season, with bright boughs and wreaths of greenery along the doorways and arches. Golden ornaments in the shapes of suns and stars adorned many a small bush or tree, along with bright red and purple ribbons.

Small children tugged on the hands of their parents as they walked, aware that the holiday meant that they, together with the Lord of Misrule and the servants, would be in charge during the celebration. Sounds of gaiety filled the air as some families had already started exchanging gifts of small candles and earthenware toys.

With a smile, Hadrian remembered his own childhood and how his parents had doted on him and his siblings, presenting them with gifts and playfully following their commands and those of the household servants. Even the slaves would be free to rule for these few days, allowing for a sense of relaxation for all during the holidays.

His recollections spurred him onward, but the closer he got to the western end of the Forum, the denser the crowd grew. He was forced to slip and slide his way past until he could no longer move forward. The people were packed shoulder-to-shoulder to watch the ceremonies ushering in the Saturnalian festivities. Many wore simpler garments than the toga in which he still dressed.

While his head was bare, felt and paper caps

adorned the heads of many, and as he exchanged a glance with one reveler, the man handed him a cap to wear. Hadrian thanked him and passed the man a small coin in exchange.

He searched the crowd for any sign of Maximillian, who was supposed to be waiting by the Temple of Vespasian. Sure enough, halfway up the stairs to that building was his friend, wearing a felt cap gaily embroidered with red and purple ribbons. Beside him were two attractive women. One of them leaned close to Maximillian and draped more ribbons around his neck.

Hadrian worked his way to his friend, while on the steps of the Temple of Saturn a gathering of senators waited. Beyond the six pillars along the portico rested the statue of Saturn, whose feet were bound with linen splints. Shortly they would be released to begin the festivities.

He had barely reached Maximillian when the cry came from the temple steps, *"Io Saturnalia!"* The cry was repeated by the crowd below and people streamed forward to partake of the feast that would be available in the temple.

The rush forward cleared the way for him.

Within a few minutes he was at Maximillian's side, but he realized now that the woman who had been artfully decorating his friend with ribbons was actually a man. A slender feminine youth who was taking advantage of the holiday liberation to cross-dress, a common practice.

"Maximillian, I see that you're ready for the season," Hadrian teased, well aware of his friend's fascination with young men. He glanced in the direction of the other person with Maximillian and his friend. Relief flooded him as he realized it was a woman. A rather attractive one at that.

Her alabaster skin seemed almost translucent. Her sable black hair was swept back from her face with ornate silver combs inlaid with mother-of-pearl. The severe look emphasized her classic features. A strong line of kohl added an Egyptian cast to her almond-shaped eyes.

She smiled and tilted her head in welcome. "I'm Stacia…and you?"

"Hadrian."

Maximillian wrapped an arm around each of them. With a boisterous greeting, he said, "So good that you know each other now. It'll spare you so many unnecessary niceties."

Which meant that Maximillian wanted to skip the feast in the temple and find a place where they would begin the Saturnalian holiday with some carnal pleasures.

He met Stacia's gaze and found amusement there, rather than upset. A paid courtesan? he wondered, but didn't stop to question it further as

Stacia shifted quickly from Maximillian's side and slipped her arm through Hadrian's.

Together they strolled away from the temple, heads bent close as Hadrian tried to find out more about his beautiful companion.

"How do you know Maximillian?" he asked and inhaled deeply as her scent teased him. She smelled of orange blossoms, fragrant and fresh.

A coy shrug shifted the simple white robe she wore, exposing the enticing slope of her full breast. "I don't really know him, but Gaius does."

He sneaked a peek over his shoulder to where Maximillian and the man he assumed to be Gaius strolled behind them, already kissing and caressing one another. Coughing, he earned a disgruntled sound from his friend.

"Seek your own pleasures, Hadrian."

His own pleasures, he thought, examining his companion again from his greater height. Bending his head close, he whispered in her ear, "What is your pleasure, Stacia? Shall we dine first?"

She surprised him by facing him and slipping her hand beneath the edge of his toga. She cupped his pectoral muscle and rubbed her thumb across the tip of his nipple. It beaded instantly and between his legs arousal slowly flared to life. Looking up at him from beneath half-lidded eyes, Stacia said, "I know a place where we can dine and…become friends."

A playful tweak of his nipple completed the job of bringing his erection to full arousal, and in his mind, he could picture them dining together. Feeding each other as they satisfied other needs, as well.

"Lead the way," he said.

The building to which Stacia led them was a richly appointed villa. As she walked to the door, a servant stepped from within and bowed at Stacia's approach.

"Mistress," the young woman said.

"Bring a meal to the baths," Stacia replied, taking the lead and keeping a hold on his hand, pulling him along behind her.

The home was lusciously appointed and clearly that of someone belonging to the patrician class. She must have noticed his gawking since she said over her shoulder, "My father was a senator."

"Was?" he said even as they stepped into the room for the baths. Colorful mosaic tiles adorned the walls, floors and the assorted pools. Wisps of steam rose from the waters and the smell of oranges was strong—the aroma that had clung to Stacia's skin, enticing him earlier. Pots with neatly trimmed orange trees, some of them ripe with fruit, were placed at regular intervals along the walls.

She released his hand and he thought that she might have changed her mind, until she shrugged off the simple tunic she wore, exposing the fine, straight line of her back. When she faced him, heat and desire raced through his body, making his erection nearly painful.

Stacia might be petite, but her body was all delicious womanly curves. Her full breasts tilted upward, dark caramel nipples large and beginning to tighten as his gaze settled on them.

Hadrian shot an uneasy look toward Maximillian and Gaius, but they were eagerly moving to a pool at a far corner of the baths, basically leaving him alone with Stacia.

Relief washed over him. Unlike Maximillian, Hadrian wasn't inclined to sexual acts in public. The two men were far enough away, however, for him to enjoy himself with the obviously uninhibited Stacia, who was trailing a toe through the water in the nearest pool. As she realized she had his attention, she smiled and moved one hand lazily up her body until she cupped her own breast.

Between his legs his erection jerked and swelled.

When she touched her beaded nipple, she asked, "Do you want to touch?"

From behind him came a series of soft footfalls, alerting him to the arrival of Stacia's servant. The young woman scurried to the side of the bath, where she placed a platter with dishes piled with fresh fruits, cheese and gold-gilded pastries drenched with honey. Just as quickly, she rushed out. As she did so, Stacia seized on the opportunity to approach him, her hips swaying enticingly.

She stopped barely inches away, one hand still working her breast. She slipped her other hand beneath the folds of his toga and unerringly found him. With a practiced touch, she caressed the tip of him and then slipped her hand over his foreskin.

He stood there, hands controlling the urge to reach for her as—with sure strokes—she sent desire rocketing through his body.

Connie let out a rough laugh, still battling the unusual need he had awakened in her body. "So you expect me to believe you just stood there while she—"

"I'm a man. I didn't just stand there, but I felt… a strange sensation moving over me. Rousing need so strong—"

"Like what you did to me," she said and finally glanced down at her body and the evidence of her own arousal. Beneath the slick black fabric, her nipples were still beaded into tight points and she was so wet between her legs, she wondered if he could smell her arousal.

"I can," he said. He laid a hand on her thigh, slowly traced it up to the rounded curve of her hip, where he encircled her waist and shifted closer on the bed. "I can smell the musk of you. It's enticing."

"It's not real," she mocked. "It's just a product of whatever you did to me."

"And you think that's not real?"

She sensed a challenge in his words. She tried to deflect it, fearful of how he intended to prove her wrong.

"Was what she did to you real? Did it please you?"

He moved the hand at her waist to just below her breast and her heart skipped a beat. She knew he heard it, sensed the way her body jumped in anticipation, the vampire thrall controlling her desire. Wanting fulfillment against her will.

With a harsh smile, he met her gaze and asked, "Do you think it pleased me?"

Chapter 6

Rome
307 A.D.

Demand raced along his nerve endings, so strong it weakened his knees as Stacia continued to pleasure him with her hand.

"What is this?" he asked, nearly light-headed from the sensations buffeting his body.

"Come, my love. Have some nourishment. You will need it before the night is through," Stacia said. With a final caress of his arousal, she turned and walked to the steps of the bath, where she waited for him.

Hadrian followed despite his better judgment, which was telling him all was not right. He had no will left to fight that sound advice. His mind was overwhelmed with the need to bury himself between Stacia's plush thighs. To feel the lush curves of her accepting his body, and taste the sweet caramel tips of her breasts.

He groaned and grabbed himself, trying to tame the heat of his cock with a few slow strokes as he walked toward her.

She smiled as she watched him caress himself. Her smile broadened as he shrugged off his toga and stood before her, all hard and eager male. She finally stopped playing with her breast and laid both her hands on his chest, stroking the muscles there. Her hands slightly chilled as she trailed them down his body, across the ridged planes of his abdomen and to the thick muscles of his thighs, avoiding the one place where he wanted her hands the most.

Urging him closer, the hard tips of her breasts brushed his chest and he moaned, wanting the taste he had imagined earlier.

"I want a taste, too." She leaned forward and placed her lips on his nipple. Sucked at it before pulling on it with her teeth.

He gasped and grabbed hold of her waist with one hand, while in his other, he tightened his hold on his erection, fighting off his release.

She laid her hand over his and, feeling the first hint of his climax, she smiled and said, "I want a taste of that as well."

Before he could stop her, she dropped to her knees and took him into her mouth, sucking and pulling at him. Unmanning him as she cupped him and squeezed gently. His release came and immediately after arousal rose up faster and harder than before. His heart slammed against the walls of his chest. He swayed on his feet until she rose up against him, her body sinuous and supportive at the same time.

"What is this?" Hadrian asked, his mind whirling from the nonstop attack on his senses. It seemed to him that he could feel every inch of her skin. The ripple of muscle beneath all that pale alabaster perfection. The intense warmth of the water as she guided him down the steps and into the heat of the baths.

A moment later he was sitting on a small ledge beneath the water and Stacia was straddling him, her thighs encircling his waist. Her breasts brushing his chest as she reached past him to the plate of food the servant had brought earlier.

She picked up one of the gilded sweets and brought it to his mouth, offering up the honey-laden treat.

When he bit down, the sweetness of the dessert filled his mouth, but then his gaze drifted downward to her breasts. His mouth watered at the sight of them, and with a laugh, Stacia rose up and offered herself to him.

"Have a taste, love. Tell me if I am as sweet."

A rush of heat swept over her body as Hadrian's gaze focused on her breasts. Connie hadn't thought it possible, but her nipples tightened into even harder nubs and throbbed with need. Between her legs a heavy pulse beat. As she pulled at the ties binding her to the posts, he said, "Do not struggle so."

The rumble in his voice dragged her gaze back to his face. His recounting of the meeting with the vampire had aroused him as well. His eyes had begun to bleed out to the penetrating neon color and a small hint of fang protruded from beyond his top lip. As she glanced downward, the fabric of his expensive slacks tented over a rather exceptional erection.

He took a shaky breath, clearly battling his own arousal. She challenged him. "Did you struggle, too, Hadrian, or did you embrace her darkness?"

A harshly uttered word—some kind of expletive, she guessed—escaped from his lips before he drove back the vampire and his human form was in control.

"When I saw her true face, I fought her, much as I expect you will fight me."

"Damn right," she said with an emphatic nod.

"But she turned me, much as I will turn you when the moment is right."

Fear replaced desire, the chill of it driving away the earlier heat of her thrall-induced arousal.

"I won't go so easily," she warned and was surprised to see a pleased smile erupt across his features. The kind of smile she hadn't expected to see in response to her challenge.

He must have sensed that she was attracted despite herself. "You are bold, aren't you?"

She was spared answering when a knock came at the door.

"Come in, George," he called out and the man from before hurried in, bringing with him a small serving cart. On the cart were two golden goblets, an open bottle of wine, some slices of bread and a dish filled with an assortment of cheeses and cold meats.

"I took the liberty earlier of assuming you might get hungry."

Connie assumed that she was like the proverbial Thanksgiving turkey and Hadrian's concern was more for keeping her nice and plump than for her comfort.

"What if I don't want to eat?"

She hated that she sounded childish to her own ears and that her response dragged another amused smile to his lips.

"Whatever. You may go, George. Have a nice night."

George, who looked to be a man not past his fifties and in relatively fine shape, glanced from her to his master and to the plate of food. Wringing his hands, he said, "You might rest easier with a little something in your belly, miss."

George had an accent, she surmised. Not quite British, but not American, either. With a shake of her head, she replied, "I won't make it easier for him, George."

"You'd be wise to make it easier on yourself," Hadrian said. With a sharp slash of his hand, he sent his servant away.

"And why is that?"

"You want to be strong enough to fight me, don't you?"

She recognized that he was playing her, but she also was smart enough to realize that she wasn't at full strength, either. Besides the arousal draining her body, he had fed from her earlier, weakening her system. She would have to feed to sustain herself until…

"You fed from me before, but I'm not a vampire."

"There are many kinds of kisses I can bestow." As he spoke, he reached for a bit of bread, dipped it into a small bowl and offered it up to her.

The rich aromas of the yeasty bread and olive oil assailed her senses and her stomach growled in reaction.

"Mangia," he said.

"It would be easier if you released me." She ate

the bread from his hand, however, savoring the rich flavors that exploded in her mouth from the morsel.

"But it's been too long a time since I indulged in such luxuries." He picked up a piece of cheese and popped it into his own mouth before snaring a small chunk for her and bringing it to her lips.

"Since your tryst with the vampire?" she asked before accepting his offering.

His hand wavered above a piece of prosciutto he had been forking onto a slice of bread. As he met her gaze, there was a wealth of sadness in his. His words when they came were unexpected and heavy with sorrow.

"Not since the day my wife and son were murdered."

Chapter 7

A ripple of shock tore across her body. "Murdered?"

Hadrian nodded and prepared her yet another bite, but when he tried to feed it to her, she clamped her lips shut and moved her head away. Her gaze was hard with judgment.

How many times had he looked in a mirror and imagined he saw the same telling stare on his own face?

Ignoring her, he poured some wine and took a sip. He offered her some as well before he popped another piece of bread and cheese into his mouth and chewed slowly, considering how to begin. How to explain how he had lost all that was ever valuable to him and why it was that he detested the humans around him.

Instead, he said, "It is too late to tell that tale. Dawn will be here in just another hour or so."

She looked in the direction of the windows, where it was still black as night outside, and when she turned a questioning glance his way, he said, "I can feel it coming, much as I can sense the approach of night."

"Is that all you can feel, Hadrian? Don't you care about your murdered family?"

"Enough." He knew her challenge was an attempt to alter the dynamic of their situation. She still hoped he might change his mind about turning her. He refused to let her get the upper hand. Rising, he paced before the bed for a moment before he asked, "And what of you, Connie? Will your family lament your passing?"

"Of course." She yanked on the ties holding her to the bed. "Why are you doing this?"

"Why?" He stalked back to the bed, grabbed hold of her chin and forced her face upward. Bending until he was nearly nose-to-nose with her, he transformed once again. Beneath his hand, her body trembled, but her gaze remained firmly on his face and gave away not a hint of her fear.

"A vampire changed my life, but it was the humans who stole all that mattered to me."

"So this is payback for something I had nothing to do with? For something I couldn't control?"

A strangled laugh escaped him. He trailed the edges of his fangs along the fine line of her jaw and the trembling of her body increased beneath his hand. When he reached the shell of her ear, he said, "Would you not kill me if you had the chance?"

Her failure to answer spoke volumes. She would kill him just for being a vampire. Just for being different. She was no different from the humans who had murdered his family and thousands of other vampires so many centuries earlier.

Thrusting her away, he rose again and said, "We will soon lie down to rest through the day. It is time to prepare for that."

Connie hadn't known what Hadrian intended to do to ready for his daytime slumber. It had turned out to be far less onerous than she had imagined.

He had let her eat and drink some more and then had untied her from the bedposts, using his vampire powers to control her while giving her the freedom to perform some nighttime ablutions in the bathroom. He had also provided her a soft silk tunic to replace the thermal undergarments she had been wearing.

The caress of the silk against her skin was almost painful to parts still in overdrive from the arousal Hadrian had awakened in her earlier. As the smooth silk slipped over her body, it had been like a lover's caress and brought fresh need.

When she had stepped out of the bathroom, Hadrian had clearly sensed her arousal. He, too, had changed into a similar garment, and as he examined her, the push of his erection against the light fabric had been obvious.

He had done nothing about it, much to her confusion.

Instead, he had bound her to the bed once again in a way that allowed her some comfort, but not the ability to untie herself. She had been hoping to attempt an escape while he slept, but sensed that even if she had done so, it would have been wasted effort.

So she lay down next to him, her body thrumming with unfulfilled need, as his was. Stiff and unyielding, much as he was. Beneath the softly decadent sheets and the silken covers, she grew warm. Beside her, Hadrian was warm as well, but as the sun rose, spilling soft rays of light into the farthest portion of the room, all warmth fled his body.

With the barest touch of light filtering through the windows, she took the time to examine the room.

Definitely masculine, she thought, glancing around at the various pieces of furniture. Large, dark and made of rich mahogany. Old World, she decided as her eyes made out the patterns on the lush fabric curtains and upholstery on the furniture.

Thick Oriental carpets were scattered across the parquet floor.

The surfaces of the various pieces of furniture were dust-free and as she inhaled, the aroma of lemon teased her nostrils. The gleaming tops of the small occasional tables and dresser held assorted mementos, all of them a testament to his apparent wealth and travels. Ornate silver candlesticks. A Fabergé egg. On the far wall what looked like a triptych of marquetry featuring various countrysides.

On the dresser closest to the bed were a smattering of silver frames, inlaid with what looked like onyx and mother-of-pearl. She wished for more light so that she might see what photos were in the frames and learn more about the demon resting beside her.

Having finished her perusal of the room, she turned her attentions to him, considering all that he had revealed during the long course of the night.

He hated humans. He had said as much. She wondered if any vestiges of humanity remained within him or if the demon had taken it all.

The demon who she suspected Hadrian hated as well. She didn't know how she knew that, but it seemed to her that for all his talk about the kind of life his vampire lover had given him, he was also angry about it. Angry and possibly full of regret.

Would she feel that way if he turned her?

Or did he just plan to drain her dry? She recalled his last words to her about whether her family would lament her passing.

Had his family lamented him?

She shifted in bed to face him. He had a Roman nose. Long and straight. Aquiline, some might say. His skin had an olive cast that last night had had a hint of color, but with the advent of the day, any and all traces of that flush of life had vanished.

That thought grabbed her attention and she glanced at the bedcovers over him, searching for any sign of breath. A very slow rise and fall, much slower than that of a human. Almost as if he were in deep hibernation.

Returning her perusal to his face, her gaze lingered on his full lips, relaxed in sleep. Dare she say that there was even a hint of a smile there?

Did vampires dream?

Below the mouth that enticed her touch was a chin with just the hint of a cleft.

So handsome, she thought again and shook her head.

She clearly had lacked for male companionship for far too long if she was actually attracted to this psycho bloodsucker.

Her friends in the office would tease her that this was what she got for spending too much time working and not allowing herself a chance to play.

Even the week she had taken for Christmas vacation had been selected primarily because she knew it would be a slow time of year at the office.

It occurred to her then that since she was off, no one would notice her disappearance for days. By the time anyone did, it would be too late for the police to find her and stop Hadrian.

At that thought, she pulled on the bindings, but she only tightened the fabric ties at her wrists.

Frustration brought tears to her eyes, but she battled them back.

Now was not the time for tears or indecision.

Using the bindings to hoist herself upward, she examined the knots he had made and realized that the only way to be free of them would be to chew through them.

Hadrian's earlier words suddenly filled her brain. *I can feel it coming, much as I can sense the approach of night.*

I'd better start chewing, Connie thought.

Chapter 8

The warmth of her, soft and female, crept into his consciousness along with the call of the night.

He opened his eyes to find their legs in a jumble and his arm across her waist.

Connie was asleep beside him, her hands still tied, but he could see threads sticking out at odd angles. She had tried to gnaw through the bindings.

He admired her spirit.

As he pulled away the bedcovers, he also couldn't avoid admiring the lush curves of her body, made more obvious by the way the silk clung to her. The fine creamy fabric also exposed the dark aureoles of her nipples.

He itched to touch. To taste.

In his dreams he had done both and more. A smile came to his face as he recalled those dreams.

"You're not so scary when you smile," she said, the tone of her voice husky with sleep.

He forced the smile away, although her words only made him want to smile even more.

"Scary is good," he said, and to prove his point, he called forth the demon.

She didn't react outwardly, although he heard the slightly faster beat of her heart. Where their legs were still intertwined, his skin was chilled before she seemed to realize the intimacy of their position and untangled her legs from his.

He missed her presence immediately and morphed back to his human form, wanting to return to that earlier sense of comfort. It had been so long since he had felt anything like it.

"Tell me a little about yourself," he said, aware that he knew nothing about her other than the fact that she was a lawyer.

"There's nothing to tell. I'm an ordinary person—"

"With an ordinary life?"

"Boring compared to what you must have seen in your long existence."

"Tell me anyway." He was eager to hear about the stuff of ordinary life.

"You miss being human, don't you?" she asked and shifted in bed. When she did, she moaned and a grimace crossed her features.

An unwelcome and hardly experienced emotion rose up in him—guilt. "Are you—"

"Okay? I'm tied to a bed and sometime today I'm going to become your meal. How okay is that?" she said, each word escalating in volume. She jerked roughly against the ties, biting her lip to hold back any outbursts of pain.

Hadrian observed her struggles and said, "If I free your hands—"

"What will I give you? What do I have that you couldn't take without asking?"

She was right that he could take all that he wanted, but what he wanted most he didn't want to take.

"I want to kiss you."

Connie nearly recoiled. Not just from the request, but from the thread of need laced through his voice.

"A kiss?" She stared hard at him, trying to read his face for confirmation of the emotions she had heard.

Unlike the hard and dispassionate cast to his features she'd seen that first night, tonight his face was alive with sentiment. The dark of his eyes glittered and a small grin peeked from one edge of his lips. The grin broadened as he seemed to realize he had her complete attention.

"A kiss? Where?" she asked.

"Wherever I want."

His gaze settled on her lips before skipping downward to her breasts, where his gaze lingered.

Heat raced through her body and her nipples tightened in response. She shifted, attempting to ease her discomfort, but the gentle glide of the fabric only increased her distress.

"So may I?" He shifted closer to her on the bed until their legs touched once again and the jut of his erection brushed the softness of her belly.

"May you what?" she asked as he raised his hand and cradled her cheek.

"Kiss you. A simple kiss." The words came as a mere whisper, low and urgent, strumming alive a need between her legs. Then he passed the pad of his thumb across her lips and said, "Here."

Her senses were on overload. She wished she could say it was because of some vampire thrall. Only she suspected it wasn't.

"You'll let me go—"

"I'll untie you…for a bit." He shifted his thumb to the line of her cheek, his caress delicate, and trained his gaze on her lips.

Being free, even if only for just a moment, would be heaven.

And it was just one little kiss, she told herself as she nodded and he closed the distance between them.

They were body-to-body. His hard and masculine, but still chilled from the night. She ignored that immortal tell as he bent his head toward her.

He hesitated and his gaze locked with hers. Seeking what? she wondered. Acceptance? Acquiescence?

But then he closed his eyes and made the first tentative pass of his lips across hers. She did the same, torn between ignoring and acknowledging the kiss. But as he passed his chilled lips across hers once again it was impossible to ignore him.

Connie gave herself over to his simple kiss, meeting his lips again and again until his were warm. Wet as she opened her mouth and accepted the slide of his tongue across them before he slipped it into her mouth.

He groaned then, a very human sound that reverberated through her body.

He had dropped his hand back to her waist. As they continued kissing, he applied gentle pressure to bring their bodies even closer, until her breasts were pressed to his chest and his arousal was impossible to miss.

She sucked in a shaky breath as she battled with herself. She shouldn't respond to all that blatant and perfect masculinity melded to her. To the gifted mouth and tongue that were turning that initial simple kiss into the kind longtime lovers shared.

Only they weren't lovers and as something

nipped her bottom lip, sharp and threatening, it reminded her of just why that was an impossibility.

He muttered a curse and shifted away. As he did so, she noted the hint of fang and the bright crimson of her blood where he had accidentally cut her. When she met his eyes, the regret in them roused an emotion she didn't want to admit.

"You hate this as much as you hate the part of you that still desires a human," she said, trying to create needed distance between them. Both because the kiss had been too tempting and because she wanted to understand the complex creature that he was.

Hadrian's reaction was swift.

He undid the wraps around her wrists. When her hands were free of the bindings, he glanced down at them and noted the raw pink sections where the silk had bitten into her skin during her struggles. He passed his fingers over them gently before looking upward and encountering her confused gaze.

"I made a promise, which I intend to keep. Do not mistake that for kindness, because it will be a grievous error."

Her hand slipped over his, her touch consoling. It might have hurt less if she had staked him. He pulled his hands away abruptly, but that didn't seem to dissuade her.

She cradled his cheek and passed her thumb across his lips, still moist and warm from their kiss.

To his surprise, she traced the fang that had nipped her, seemingly unfazed by its presence. When her gaze locked on his, she said, "Tell me why you hate so much, Hadrian."

To his surprise, he did.

Rome
311 A.D.

It had been nearly four years since that fateful Saturnalian tryst had taken one existence and provided him with another. He had hated Stacia at first, confused as he was by what she had made him and all that had seemed forbidden to him after his transformation.

He was no longer human and all things human seemed beyond his reach.

Even something as simple as a daytime walk was no longer possible, although he had discovered that by the very late afternoon hours he could venture out.

To compensate for his new existence, he lost himself in endless hours of work during the day and meaningless nighttime trysts meant to satisfy the new desires that rose up in him, sometimes beyond his control.

When on one occasion he had nearly drained a woman to death, he swore off human feedings and instead subsisted only on beef and pig blood.

Despite that, the urge to sink his teeth into human flesh proved to be a temptation, so he shut himself off from others, even from his family. Thanks to Maximillian, who had also been turned that fateful night, Hadrian found a keeper who tended to his feedings and other needs.

In time he learned control, and control brought him an unexpected gift—a wife.

Anastasia had been a teen when he had first met her—the daughter of one of his father's friends. She had grown into a beautiful young woman before his eyes and on those occasions when he had involved himself with family, she had caught his attention. He discovered that he had also caught hers.

But what had intrigued him more than her beauty had been her wit and independence. His hope that the latter might somehow make her more understanding of his condition proved true, and after a rather short courtship, he married her. Barely six months later and hopelessly in love, he had turned her after discovering that Anastasia was dying from consumption.

The transformation he had hated now brought him eternal life with his beloved wife, but it also brought an unexpected gift—a son.

Anastasia had been fertile when he had turned her and bedded her. The sweeping physical changes caused by becoming a vampire had allowed for the conception of a child—a human child.

They named him Justus and his family lived happily in one of the neighborhoods in Rome that had become a mecca for others like them—vampires living relatively normal lives.

But then the rumors started. Just one or two at first, but they grew with alarming speed. A small but extremist sect within Emperor Constantine's sun-worshippers had decided to eradicate the elements of darkness they viewed as a threat.

Vampires were being dragged off the streets. Families were pulled out of their homes and carted off in wagons, which were left to sit in the open so that the vampires would roast beneath the sun's rays.

Hadrian ignored the rumors at first, thinking that they were just wild talk, although he sensed the undercurrents at his business and elsewhere. People were being more careful about with whom they consorted. Constantine was taken with the new religion and meant to firmly defend it when he could. Those extremists within his fold intended to take it a step further, punishing any who were nonbelievers.

Hadrian had even seen one attack himself just a few doors down from his shop in the *Forum Vinarium*. One of the other wine merchants, a practicing pagan, had been nearly beaten to death by a gang of young sun-worshippers. He had helped the old man back into his shop and realized that it was time to consider moving his family to the large country villa his father owned.

He sent word for the villa to be prepared and ordered his keeper to make sure it would be suitable for their needs.

Unfortunately, he had waited too long to make the move.

Chapter 9

"I found my wife and son hanging from the portal of our home, which had been set on fire."

Hadrian's hands were clenched tightly in his lap and Connie placed one hand over his. "Justus was just a boy."

"But tainted by having a vampire mother." To her surprise, he turned his palm upward and grasped her hand as he continued his story.

"I wanted to cut them down, bury them. Only Constantine's thugs had returned, eager for more bloodshed. So I ran to my father's, thinking it would be safe there."

He tightened his hand on hers. His gaze glittered

with unshed tears. His voice, when he continued, had a husky note from the emotions he tried to suppress. Emotions that were limning the dark brown irises of his eyes with the shocking glow of the demon.

"They were all dead. My mother and father. My younger brother and sister, barely into their teens. Slaughtered because of me."

Connie cradled his cheek. "Not because of you. It was because those thugs were afraid of something that was different from them."

"Don't all humans have the same fear? Wouldn't you stake me if you could?"

"I'm not like that. I—"

"Could accept what I am?" he challenged with a sardonic arch to his brow, all traces of his earlier vulnerability walled up behind the stony features of his face.

Could she? Connie wondered, running her thumb across his lips. Human lips right now, but in her mind's eye came the recollection of his lethal fangs. Of the nip at her lip and the sharp bite of pain from last night.

Slowly she withdrew her touch. He was more right than she cared to admit, having always thought herself rather liberal and unprejudiced at heart.

Her encounter with Hadrian was proving her wrong on so many levels.

His lips curled in a mocking grin, but before he could rebuke her, a knock came at the door.

At Hadrian's bidding, George entered the room, wheeling the now almost-familiar cart. If he found it odd that she was free and sharing Hadrian's bed, he said nothing. He merely took the cart to the far side of the room and the small table she had noted earlier. He quickly transferred the contents of the cart to the table and left the room.

"Are you hungry?" Hadrian asked even as he was moving from the bed to the table, the loose folds of his tunic falling to just above his knee, exposing the defined muscles of his legs.

She rose as well and joined him, the slide of the silk sensuous on her skin. He watched her as she approached, hunger in his gaze.

Human hunger.

Inside of her, something awakened with that look, contradicting her earlier thoughts that she couldn't accept what he was. When he looked like this—admired her like this—it made it easier to forget that he was a demon who had sucked her blood. Who intended to suck her dry unless...

She convinced him she was different. Would that be enough? she wondered, but as she recalled his dislike of the bell and the Santa suit, she suspected it might not be.

She had to find out what would be enough because the answer could be the means to her salvation.

At the edge of the table, he behaved as any well-mannered gentleman might. He pulled out the chair for her, but instead of sitting across from her, he took a place right at her side. Like a lover.

He served her cheeses, prosciutto, olives and assorted vegetables from a small antipasto tray. The smells were sharp and earthy, in contrast to the yeasty aroma from the bread nearby. He passed her a crusty slice before serving himself some of the food.

She remembered seeing him eat the night before and wondered aloud, "Vampires eat?"

With a shrug, Hadrian speared a piece of *grana* and popped it into his mouth. As he chewed he said, "It brings no sustenance, but we can still savor the taste."

"So do you eat food often or only when you have guests?"

He had been dipping a peace of bread into the olive oil from the vegetables. He stopped mid-dip. "I don't have guests—"

"You have meals?"

Hadrian chuckled and resumed dipping. "If by meals you mean humans, then the answer is 'no.'"

"So you have guests—"

"I don't have guests. Ever. Now eat," he said and punctuated the statement by popping an olive into his mouth.

Connie recalled his words from the night before

about keeping up her strength. He wanted her to eat and be strong so that he would be satisfied when he fed.

Even though she had been hungry, she pushed away her plate.

"I've lost my appetite."

"Coward. Somehow I expected more from you, being a fellow bloodsucker and all." He kept on eating, seemingly undisturbed.

"I'm not in top form this week. Chalk it up to being on vacation. Some vacation it turned out to be."

Hadrian examined her as she sat beside him, her hands held together in her lap. Her face downcast. "Christmas vacation, I gather."

She nodded and her thick swath of hair shifted back and forth with the movement, obscuring his view. He reached up and tucked it behind her ear, needing to see her expressive face. "Tell me what you had planned to do."

A shrug sent the shift slipping off one shoulder, exposing the creamy skin of her upper arm. He ran a finger along the line of her shoulder and she shivered from his touch.

"Am I that disgusting?"

With a quick look in his direction, she said, "It depends."

He had no doubt what it depended on. "If I promise to stay human, will you eat?"

A furrow formed above her eyes as she considered him, confusion and something else lingering in her gaze.

"That would make it easier for you, wouldn't it?" he said.

The furrow deepened as did her confusion. "Easier? How?"

He stroked the ridge of her collarbone with his thumb and then dropped it a bit lower to just above the swell of her breasts. Another shiver danced along her body, different this time.

"It would make it easier for you to deal with this…need. With your attraction to me."

He dared to drop his hand a little lower and passed his thumb across the taut peak of her nipple. The shudder that ripped through her body this time was stronger. The gasp escaping her lips left no doubt about his effect on her.

"You don't want to enjoy my darkness."

"No," exploded from her lips as he took her nipple between his thumb and forefinger, and rotated it gently.

If the truth were told, he didn't want to desire her, either. She was goodness and light and, worst of all, human. Needing her could bring him nothing but more pain during yet another dismal Christmas season.

He had to drag his hand from her breast. Pull

himself away from wanting to remove the shift she wore. He wanted to explore the rest of her. Savor the warmth and life pulsing beneath her skin. Plunge into the hot, wet depths of her femininity and hear her cry his name as he drove into her.

"I see that I'm not the only one who doesn't want this," she said, her gaze dropping below his waist for a moment before locking with his.

"No, I don't," he said.

"So what does that make us, Hadrian?" she asked and her name on his lips tightened his gut, swelling an already painful arousal.

"Crazy," he admitted, yanking a bemused chuckle from her.

He turned away from her and faced the table once again, where he cleared away their dirty plates and prepared for the next course. Reaching for another of the platters George had brought, he spooned delicate strands of cappellini in an almond pesto cream sauce onto their dishes. When he was done, he gestured to the pasta with his hand and said, "Eat."

She did. Hesitantly at first, but after a few sips of her wine, she attacked the meal with gusto until the plate before her was clean.

"That was good," she said and he nodded in agreement.

"George's wife is quite a good cook."

"George has a family?" she asked and snared another piece of bread from the basket.

"He lives on the lower three floors with them in exchange for his care of me."

Connie was about to say that it was some gig to have a ritzy East Side brownstone in exchange for being a caretaker until she thought about what else a caretaker might need to do—like dispose of Hadrian's leftovers. Except he had said he didn't ever have guests here.

"Am I the only...dinner you've brought home with you?"

He chuckled. "Now that's the spirit that intrigued me."

As he cleared away the plates once again, she pressed her point. "Am I or does George get to take out your trash as part of his responsibilities?"

He paused in the act of setting the plate before her. "You're the only human who I've brought into my home."

The plate thunked onto the table before her and with jerky motions, he spooned out yet another course—chunks of tender veal swimming in a brown sauce.

"You've yet to really tell me anything about yourself," he said.

With a shrug, she reminded him, "Like I said before, I'm rather ordinary."

He trained his gaze on her, dark and demanding. When he spoke, the tones of his voice were low, like a lover's in the middle of the night. "You're anything but ordinary, Connie. But I suspect you already know how beautiful you are."

She didn't, actually. She had never been the kind to put much faith in her looks, choosing instead to rely on her intelligence and other abilities to get ahead. It occurred to her in that moment that if he found her beautiful seduction could accomplish what intelligence hadn't so far.

"Maybe it's not something all the men in my life make a point of telling me," she said, which wasn't far from the truth. Well, maybe a bit of a stretch since she could count the men who had been in her life on one hand. Okay, maybe not even her whole hand, just three fingers, she thought.

A wry smile quirked the edges of his lips. "You're not a very good liar."

"Why do you say that?" She ate a bit of the veal and found the flavor rich. The gravy had bits of mushroom, intensifying the richness of the dish.

"I suspect you haven't had many men in your life. But I won't be put off if you try and prove me wrong."

She dropped her fork onto her plate, where it clattered against the expensive bone china and sent a bit of gravy flying onto the white linen tablecloth. "Excuse me? Prove you wrong?"

He placed his own fork down more carefully and turned in his chair to face her.

"Yes, prove me wrong. Seduce me."

Chapter 10

*S*educe him.

With him in his human state, it wouldn't be such a hard task. He was more than attractive. He was drop-dead gorgeous. With his being a vampire, however, those words took on whole new meaning.

Not to mention that her experience with men was limited. She had never played the role of the seductress. Never thought of herself that way, but if that was what it would take to earn her freedom...

She drove away the concern about what she would do if along the way she came to feel something for him.

First step, touch him, she told herself.

He had an unruly lock of hair that sometimes drifted down over his forehead. She reached out and swept it back, saying as she did so, "You'd like me to seduce you."

He laid his hand on her upper arm and lazily stroked her skin. "It's been a long time since a woman as intriguing as you has enticed me."

Her gaze locked with his and she found no deception about his feelings. He desired her, but before she took this little game further, she wanted to make some things clear.

"No thrall or other vampire tricks. I want you one hundred percent human."

A frown marred his lips and she swept her hand down, passed her thumb across them. "I want that because…it needs to be real for me. I want what I feel to be real."

Hadrian thought about the many women he had lured with the vampire's pheromones over nearly two millennia. He had controlled them for one reason only—to feed. Whatever physical passion had come along for the ride had failed to move him.

But Connie moved him.

He wanted to experience more of that with her and so he nodded and shifted his hand to the fine line of her collarbone.

"One hundred percent human." Beneath his hand, the tension rushed from her body.

She dropped her hand from his face to his shoulder, where she brushed aside the shift he wore to stroke the skin beneath. He knew it would be cold to the touch and normally he summoned the vampire a bit because the transformation brought heat. But he had made a promise and he meant to keep it.

Connie stroked the muscles of his shoulder tentatively before fingering the edge of the shift.

"Do you normally wear this to bed?"

He glanced down at the garment before meeting her gaze again and shooting her a smile. "Not usually."

"Oh."

"Would you like some dessert?" he asked at the same time that she said, "Would you like to get comfortable?"

"Comfortable?" he said and she motioned to the silken shift he wore.

"Oh," he said, but decided that before she changed her mind, he would take advantage of her offer. He whipped the garment off and tossed it to the side, exposing himself.

Connie sucked in a shaky breath as she beheld all of him. Lean and powerfully built, with muscles that were nicely defined but not bulky. He had little hair on his chest, just a smattering of dark softness above his heart with a happy trail down the center of his body, past ridged abs and to...

An uncircumcised penis that had grown remarkably erect with her perusal. His foreskin hid all but the tip of his penis from her. As her gaze lingered there, he glanced down as well and with a shrug said, "It was the norm when I was born."

"Right." She jerked her attention back to the table and his earlier question. "Dessert would be lovely."

With shaky hands, he cleared the dinner plates and placed dessert before them—a mound of small deep-fried balls of dough glistening with something sweet and dotted with colored sprinkles. He picked off a few of the balls and offered them to her.

"You really have got to eat these with your fingers."

He brought them to her lips and she opened her mouth, ate them. The dough balls were crunchy and the syrup turned out to be some kind of honey glaze.

"Good," she said and watched as he licked the honey from his fingers. The motion tightened something inside of her and as he reached for more of the sweets, she stopped him. Instead, she picked up several of them and raised them to his mouth.

He glanced at them and then at her with some hesitation, but then he grasped her wrist, held her hand steady as he opened his mouth and ate the sweets. He swallowed quickly and then applied gentle pressure to bring her hand to his lips.

Opening his mouth, he licked her index finger to

remove what remained of the syrup. Then he moved on to each of her other fingers, licking and sucking each one into his mouth.

When he released her hand she ripped it back quickly and rubbed it on her shift, but it was impossible to wipe away the feel of his mouth and tongue. It was impossible to keep from imagining how they might feel on other parts of her body and that imagining brought a very obvious response that he was quick to embrace.

"I can end the wondering, *cara*."

Nervously she rubbed her hands back and forth on the shift, feeling the silken slide of it against her skin. Imagining instead the slide of his mouth and lips.

She nodded, unable to voice her request, but he surprised her by dropping to his knees before her.

"Hadrian," she said and laid a hand on his shoulder.

His muscles rippled beneath her hand before he asked, "Say my name again, *cara*."

A simple request. Say his name.

The way she would see him as a human by just saying his name.

"Hadrian."

The muscles of his shoulder tightened for a moment and then relief washed over him.

But relief was the last thing she felt as he slipped his hand around her calf and gently raised her leg, bringing her foot to his mouth. As he had done with her fingers, he licked each toe. Each pull of his mouth created a tug between her legs.

He moved upward, to the inside of her ankle, where he dropped a kiss and gave a lick.

She shivered, anticipating where he was headed next as he kissed her kneecap and rubbed his cheek against the inside skin there.

"I thought I was supposed to be doing the seducing?" she asked as he inched the shift upward, exposing her thighs.

He eased his body between the vee of her legs and laid his hands on her thighs, rubbing back and forth in a gentle caress. A wry smile came to his face as he asked, "Do you want me to stop?"

She was throbbing, damp between her legs. The last thing she wanted him to do was to stop, so she shook her head.

His smile broadened, but he didn't press forward. Instead, he traced an idle pattern on her thigh with his fingers. "I didn't hear you. I need to hear you say it. Say my name, *cara*."

"Not *cara*, Hadrian. Connie. My name is Connie."

A strangled laugh escaped him. "Connie. Do you want me to stop, Connie?"

"No, Hadrian. I don't want you to stop."

With gentle hands, he grasped her thighs and urged her to the edge of the chair. Tardily he dropped a series of kisses up the inside of one thigh, skipped the place she wanted him most before kissing his way back down the inside of the other thigh.

She gripped his body with her thighs and shifted restlessly on the edge of the chair, wanting his touch. Needing his hands and mouth on her. His human hands and mouth, driving home the reality that the demon had not emerged. That, as he promised, all that she was feeling was real.

Which almost made her stop. Reality would only make it more difficult to…

All thoughts fled her brain as he finally brought his mouth to the center of her, expertly finding her clitoris and kissing it, licking at it and then nibbling the nub, creating an undeniable wave of desire throughout her body.

He didn't stop there, moving to kiss and gently bite her lips until he got to the core of her. Slowly he slipped his tongue inside her.

She gasped and throbbed around him. She nearly came right then and there, but in hushed tones, he said, "Not yet, Connie. There's still much more to savor."

He bent his head to her center and once again teased the swollen nub first with his tongue and then his teeth. His mouth dragged a moan from her and her body trembled as he eased one finger inside and then a second.

Her hips lifted off the chair and Hadrian lifted up

his head, searching her face for any contradictory signs. Finding none, he eased his fingers from within her and rose, lifting the shift from her body as he did so.

He held his hand out to her, wanting her to rise, but with a husky laugh, she said, "I'm not quite sure my legs will hold me up right now. Besides, I thought I was supposed to seduce you."

She reached out and laid her hand on his erection, softly stroking it, clearly finding the foreskin of interest. Gently she traced her fingers around it and then to the tip, where the head of his penis peeked out. When she ran her finger across that sensitive tip, he grunted in pleasure.

A smile came to her face. A siren's smile showing delight at the control he had just given her.

He gave her more, placing his hand over hers, gently guiding her strokes until he was shaking from the caresses.

She surprised him then by leaning forward and placing a kiss at the tip of his penis, licking it and then applying slightly more pressure to pull back his skin and fully expose the head of him. She moistened him with her mouth and then caressed him with her hand, dragging a hoarse cry from him.

"Connie."

"Touch me, Hadrian. I want your hands on me."

She left him only long enough to urge his hands to her breasts.

Her nipples were hard little points against his palms as he rubbed his hands there. When she took him into her mouth again, he sucked in a breath and closed his eyes, giving himself over to the sensations.

Warm skin against his palms.

Tight little peaks he rotated with his fingers.

Her gasp spilled warm breath against his arousal, wet with her kisses.

He wanted more.

Reluctantly he pulled away from her, but only long enough to scoop her in his arms and take her back to the bed. He fell onto it with her beneath him. Warm, soft woman. Welcoming as she raised her thighs and cradled his hips. She opened her mouth to him as he kissed her, over and over again until he had to take her.

He found the center of her, slowly slid home and then stilled, pleasure nearly overwhelming him.

He gazed down at her. Her eyes—an amazing shade of slate—had darkened. Her pupils were wide as her gaze roamed over his face. Choppy little breaths spilled from her lips as she picked up her hand and cradled his jaw.

"Hadrian," she said as she passed her thumb across the sharp line of his cheekbone.

His gut clenched at the sound of his name on her lips. It took all of his control not to come. He didn't want to do that without pleasuring her first. Without experiencing the wonder of her, so different from anything he had allowed himself for so long.

He bent his head and kissed her again, slowly explored the contours of her lips. The warmth of her mouth and sweet slide of her tongue against his. Her taste was fresh and still sweet from the honey of the dessert.

But he knew something that might taste sweeter and left her mouth, kissing his way down to her breasts. Gently he took the tip of one into his mouth and sucked.

It was as sweet as he had thought it would be.

Connie moaned as he surrounded her nipple with his lips and gently tugged on it. She cradled his head with one hand while moving the other to the small of his back, holding him tight.

He was thick and heavy inside of her, creating a fullness that needed more. With a flex of her hips she moved him and he groaned against her breast.

"Connie."

Dios mios, she had to be insane to be wanting him so much. He was a bloodsucking demon who was going to drain her of life, she tried to remind herself, but it was hard to remember that from the gentle kisses he dropped on her breasts and the way he restrained himself as he finally began to move.

He was controlling himself, she knew. Wanting

to satisfy her as he moved his hips and caressed her breasts and dropped down to kiss her every now and then.

Connie's body was trembling and damp with her sweat, warm from the desire he roused in her. He slowly increased the pace of his thrusts until she was digging her heels into the mattress. Gripping his shoulders tightly to deepen his penetration.

His rough breath matched hers as her climax coalesced inside of her, building in intensity until with one last thrust, she came, calling out his name. She tightened her hold on him as her body shook with her release.

Hadrian stilled his motion to savor her climax. She clenched around him, nearly undoing him, but he held on, wanting the sensation of her never to end.

As her climax ebbed, he used his strength to roll onto his back and bring her to straddle him. The position drove him deep and she moaned with pleasure.

"Hadrian?" she asked, placing her hands on his chest to support herself.

"Make love to me, Connie," he said, running his hands up her arms until he reached her breasts and once again fondled them lovingly.

She jumped at that touch and sucked in a rough breath, but then she moved. Shifting her hips back and forth, drawing him in and out of her. The movement created delicious friction where they were joined.

"That's it, *cara*," he urged and moved his hands to her hips, guiding her until she climaxed again, calling out his name.

He lost it then, as his body jumped from the force of the pleasure that rushed over him.

When she dropped down on his body, he was enveloped in the experience of her. Of her warmth and the slight dampness on her skin. In the musky smells of her arousal and the tastes of her. Earthy. Sweet.

As he held her, her heart beat a frantic pace against his chest from the passion she had just experienced.

The frantic beat stirred the beast within him. The one he had promised to keep in check.

She sensed it, since she stiffened above him and pushed away from him.

Her hurt gaze seared him with condemnation, but the demon within him refused to be restrained.

As he surged forward, reversing their positions and pinning her to the mattress, he said, "I'm sorry."

Then he sank his fangs into her neck and fed.

Chapter 11

When she woke, she was tied to the bedposts again.

Her body was sore, but not from being tied. The ache was from their earlier lovemaking. Mortification rose up within her as she recalled all that she had done. All that she had let him do.

She should have known better than to trust a demon.

The last things she remembered were his apologetic words and a barely uttered promise as he bit her—"I'll never let you go."

She knew she was alive. She wondered if the fact that she was still tied to the bedposts meant he hadn't turned her, that he was keeping her around

for another meal. And then another and another—
because he didn't intend to release her.

Connie couldn't let that happen.

He wasn't in bed with her although she could tell
it was daytime by the strong light filtering around
the edges of the curtains. They had been drawn this
time and as her eyes focused, she finally saw him,
sprawled on a small sofa across the room. Probably
the reason why the curtains had been closed. Otherwise the rays of the sun would have been bathing
his body as he slept.

She wondered for only a moment why he wasn't
beside her in bed.

Guilt perhaps?

She didn't consider it further, opting to focus on
how to either undo the ties or…

The bindings were still as secure as they had
been the night before, but the other ends of the ties
were higher up on the bedposts. High enough that
she might be able to snap it off.

Connie turned so that her feet were up against the
wooden headboard, forcing her to curl into a tight
ball. All the better, she thought as she pushed off
with both her legs and arms, the ornate wood
carvings digging into the balls of her feet.

The post and headboard swayed a bit, but held fast.

Sharp, intense pressure was what she needed.

Risking a glance to see if she had disturbed him,

she realized that Hadrian slept on, apparently unaware of her escape attempt.

Bunching her thighs, she secured the position of her feet against the headboard once again and drew in a deep breath. With an intense surge of power, she jerked with all her might.

The crack of wood splintering was sweet, but the bedpost didn't completely give way.

She looked toward Hadrian again. No sign that he had heard a thing.

Her arms and legs strained as she pulled, but the groan of the wood spurred her onward. With one final tug, the post snapped and landed in her lap.

With the sharp ragged point of the bedpost, she sawed through the thinnest part of the ties. She never gave a thought to the bindings at her wrists. They were too tight and she risked slicing open her wrists if she tried. All she needed was to have her hands free.

A second later she had that wish.

During all that time, Hadrian hadn't stirred.

Quietly she crept toward the door, the pointed bedpost stake in hand for defense. But as she neared the door, she realized that she was buck naked. She couldn't leave like this. There were two doors before her and George had come and gone through one of them. She hoped the other was a closet.

Gingerly she turned the knob and peered within.

Sure enough it was a large walk-in closet. She went in and closed the door behind her, turning on a light as she did so. The room was filled with an assortment of clothing. From the jeans to the suits, all of it was of the highest quality.

He was tall and she was round. His jeans barely fit across her hips, but she had to cuff them repeatedly so she wouldn't trip over them. Snagging a black sweater from a shelf, she slipped it on over her head.

It smelled like him. Something woodsy and indefinably masculine.

Her body sprang to painful life, worrying her. Would she never be free of his presence after this chance encounter?

I will never let you go.

His words echoed in her head and she imagined him stalking her. Always present. The fear she would live with forever unless she found a way to…

Be rid of him? she wondered.

She eased out of the closet and peered toward the sofa, but he wasn't there.

A second later someone grabbed her from behind and she reacted, seizing his arm and shifting her weight.

Hadrian went up and over her shoulder to land with a thud on the floor. Before he could move, she was straddling him, the sharp point of the stake directly above his heart. An angry red scratch marred his flesh where she had scraped the bedpost stake against his skin.

She would only have to place her weight on the stake and it would pierce his heart. Just a little more pressure and...

"I can smell your fear. You want to do this, so do it."

Connie couldn't ignore the pain in his voice. "Promise you'll leave me be—"

"Do it, Connie. I'm a monster, remember. Doesn't that make it easier?"

She met his gaze and his regret slammed into her. Was it because of what he had done last night? Because he had broken his promise? *So what good would his promise do now?* she thought and yet she asked again.

"Promise to leave me be, Hadrian."

To emphasize her point, she pressed a little harder on the stake and the flesh beneath it grew white from the pressure.

Hadrian thought about never seeing her again. About the spirit and excitement she had brought into his life in just two short days. He might be better off to have her stake him rather than go back to his drab and empty existence.

He laid his hand over hers as it rested on the stake and pressed downward, experiencing the first pinch of pain as the wood pierced his flesh.

"Do it. Prove to me you are no different than all those others. The ones who killed my family and vowed to destroy my kind."

Her hand trembled beneath his and suddenly she was in motion, fleeing the room.

Her bare feet slapped against the wood of the stairs as she made her flight to freedom. The crash of the front door told him she had made her escape.

He still held the stake in his hand and for a moment, he considered driving it home. But then hope rose, stronger than it ever had before. He released the stake and sat up, staring out the open door to his bedroom.

She had asked him to make a promise. One he couldn't make. But he suspected that if he had asked her to make the same promise, she could not.

Connie would be back.

By the time Connie got home, she was ice cold. Running around barefoot and with no coat had been the only option, but the chill of the day had gotten into her bones along with another chill—that of fear.

She took a hot bath to get rid of the first, but it also helped to wipe away the smell of him on her body.

She wondered how long it would be before she could drive Hadrian out of her brain.

The hot bath made her feel lethargic. Or maybe it was the events of the past two days. The physical and mental strain. The drain Hadrian had put on her system by feeding from her.

He had broken his promise. She could never trust his word again, she thought, but just as suddenly it occurred to her that she wouldn't have to worry about that.

She never intended to see him again.

To rid herself of the tiredness in her mind and limbs, she slipped under the covers for a long nap. She only had a few hours before she would have to decide whether to go back to the Santa stint in front of the library.

Whether she dared to confront him once more.

Sleep came quickly beneath the soft embrace of the heavy covers and the heat that developed within her little cocoon. But it wasn't untroubled sleep. Over and over Hadrian's words came again as he told her about his life. She experienced his loss and sorrow, recreating the well of sympathy within her that she had experienced before he had made her his dinner.

She drove away that sympathy, wanting to maintain her anger. She needed that to deal with the conflicting emotions that continued to war within her as images slowly crept into her consciousness. Somehow she knew they weren't dream images. They were Hadrian's memories, playing out like a movie in her brain.

Showing her his final Christmas torment.

Chapter 12

Rome, 312 A.D.
December 21, Julian Calendar
December 25, Gregorian Calendar
Winter Solstice
Sol Invictus
Christmas Day

For weeks after the murder of his family, Hadrian hid where he could during the day, emerging at night only long enough to find something or someone on which to feed. He moved constantly to avoid the extremists within Constantine's fold that were still terrorizing vampires everywhere.

Then one day he took shelter in an underground tunnel used for burying the human dead. In the catacombs below the outskirts of Rome, he had stumbled upon a meeting of a vampire resistance group. They were tired of having their families murdered and hiding like animals. They were organizing. Planning a way to rid themselves of Constantine and the thugs who killed in his name.

Hadrian had no doubt he would join them. He was tired of hiding like a whipped dog and had wanted vengeance against those who had killed his family.

After months of training and waiting, their day finally arrived. Hadrian marched along with hundreds of other vampires through the catacombs to the natural caves, which would open up outside of the city.

The Red Rocks were just miles beyond Rome, surrounded by various hills and the Tiber.

Maxentius was camped there already, ready to face Constantine for control of the Western portions of the Roman Empire. The vampires had thrown in their lot with him, hopeful that Maxentius would offer them a peaceful existence within his realm.

Because of their participation, Maxentius and the vampire leaders had chosen the day of the winter solstice for their attack. The longest night of the year would give the vampire warriors more time to fight and hopefully secure a victory for Constantine's challenger.

The battle was already raging by the time the vampires streamed from below ground at dusk.

Hadrian charged out, sword and shield in hand. Cutting and slashing his way through the legions of Constantine's soldiers, he quickly realized they were greatly outnumbered. It would take all of their number and then some to win the day before the sun rose and they would have to retreat.

The ground beneath his feet was sloppy from the blood spilled during the battle. His arm grew weary, but he kept on fighting, even when blow after blow landed on him. One particularly nasty sword thrust nearly ran him through, dropping him to his knees. Excruciating pain erupted through his body as Constantine's soldier pulled his sword out, intending to complete his mission by decapitating Hadrian—one of the best ways of ensuring that Hadrian would not rise again to join the battle.

Somehow he managed to block the soldier's blow and counter with one of his own, driving the blade of his sword deep into the soldier's belly.

As the man dropped to the ground before him, Hadrian crawled to rest against a nearby rock, waiting for his vampire body to heal so he could resume the fight. Those few minutes gave him time to fully see the panorama before him. The masses of men and vampires, fighting one another. Blood spewing from wounds as body parts went flying and men dropped to the ground, either dead or dying.

Many of Maxentius's men already lay there beside their vampire comrades, killed by the hundreds of soldiers under Constantine's command. There were so many of them, Hadrian thought, dragging in a painful breath and realizing that beside the wound in his abdomen, another deep sword thrust had pierced his side. It was why he was taking so long to heal.

But he could not linger. If not for the advent of the vampires, the battle would have been lost long ago.

Slowly rising to his feet, he lunged forward to meet yet another charge from Constantine's men. Their shields sported the Greek letters *chi* and *rho*— the abbreviation for *Christos,* Constantine's new god. The two letters were superimposed on one another, recreating the martyred god on his cross.

Although pain and weariness dragged at his every move, Hadrian battled on beside others of the vampire underground. They understood this might be their last stand, but if they were going to live in freedom, they had to take this chance.

The battle raged long into the night and the vampires managed to hold their own, possibly even advance.

If Maxentius could rally his remaining human troops behind them, victory would be theirs. But even as Hadrian held on through the long solstice night, battling for his life, he knew that once the sun began to rise, he and his compatriots would need to retreat.

He told himself that was some time away, even as the faintest signs of dawn slowly crept into the sky, but then the first of those rays was caught on the bright shield of one of Constantine's men. He watched as the vampire standing before that man reeled away, the sign of the cross burned across his skin as the sun's rays were amplified by the mirror-shiny shields.

A low roar gathered strength amongst Constantine's sun worshippers, who interpreted the branding of the vampire as a sign. As if one, they turned their shields to the nascent rays of the dawn and before Hadrian's eyes, vampire after vampire turned away in pain or ran for the cover of the darkness only to be struck down even as they retreated.

Hadrian slashed his way past one soldier and held up his shield to avoid the reflected rays another was directing his way.

A blow came across his back, driving him to his knees, but he rolled away from the next killing thrust and managed to rise and slay his attacker.

But he was weakening from a combination of blood loss and the rising rays of the sun.

He would not have his vengeance, he realized as

before him vampire after vampire fell dead at the hands of the sun-worshippers. Dozens of others fled the sun and the symbol of the cross, streaming back into the caves from where they had emerged, Constantine's men in hot pursuit.

His skin began to tingle from the rising sun's rays, but he was too far away from the entrance to the caves and even if he got there, only death awaited him.

Constantine's men would not leave any of them alive.

He searched around wildly, looking for shelter, but the only things around him were death and destruction. Hundreds of humans, their blood steaming in the chill of the morning. Half as many vampires, their bodies slowly cooking beneath the sun's rays. His own skin starting to redden and ache as the sun rose higher.

A dozen feet away a small crevasse cut deeply into the hillside. He made a run for it, slashing and killing the few soldiers who had remained behind on the field. He dived into a small and narrow piece of the crevasse and pulled the bodies of the fallen above him to shield him from the sun.

It would take days for them to get to clearing the field of battle.

All he needed was a half a dozen hours or so until the sun was weaker and he could attempt an escape.

But first, he needed to feed so that he would heal. He reached for the closest body. It was still warm with life.

He sank his fangs into the dead human's neck and fed.

Connie bolted upright in bed, breathing as heavily as if she had just fought the battle for her life.

In her mind's eye came the scenes of death Hadrian had witnessed over a millennia of Christmas holidays.

No wonder he hated the festival. It had cost him so much.

So much and yet…

She recalled the tenderness of his touch and tried to reconcile it with his bloodthirstiness. Somehow it wasn't as hard to do as she might have thought.

Which made her reconsider whether she would don the Santa suit that night and remind him of his torment.

The loud buzz of the intercom made her jump.

She slipped from bed and padded to the door of her apartment, where she buzzed the doorman.

"There's a messenger for you, Ms. Morales. He says his name is George."

George. She wondered if he had come to fetch her for his master, but she wasn't about to hide out in fear.

"Please send him up."

She slipped on a robe and when the knock came, she opened the door.

George stood there, a wrapped packaged in hand. "Your things, miss. Hadrian thought you would want them."

With trembling hands she reached for the package and took it from his hands. She murmured her thanks and George tipped his head and began to walk away, but before she could close her door, he pivoted and faced her once again.

"He's not a bad sort, you know. Takes care of me and my family just fine." He reached into his pocket and withdrew a card, handed it to her. "Just in case you change your mind."

He left after that and she closed the door, staring at the card that had only a phone number on it.

Hadrian's? she wondered.

She tucked the card into the pocket of her robe, walked to her sofa and placed the package on the coffee table. The package was wrapped in plain brown paper and tied with twine.

A simple pull undid the knot, unlike the ties that had bound her. Unwrapping the paper revealed her shoes, purse and the clothing she had been wearing when Hadrian had taken her. Beneath that was another simply wrapped package.

She unwrapped it to find the Santa suit and beard,

freshly laundered and smelling way better than when she had last donned them.

A message from him? she pondered. Or an apology?

There was only one way to find out.

Chapter 13

Hadrian woke to the peal of the bell and the softly whispered greeting to a passerby. It brought a smile to his lips before regret ripped into him.

He stretched as he rose and rubbed his hand over the center of his chest. Pain lingered there, but no scar. The angry scratch and cut from the bedpost stake were long gone.

Vampires healed fairly quickly if they were healthy and well-fed. He was certainly the latter, he thought, and glanced up at the bedpost she had snapped off during her escape.

George had already started repairs. The top of the post was back in place and a lighter rim of color identified where the keeper had used some kind of wood filler to hide the damage.

A knock came at the door and at Hadrian's command to enter, George came in, wheeling the cart before him.

Hadrian sat on the edge of the bed and motioned to the patched wood. "You've started to fix the bedpost. It looks good."

George nodded, but the smile he gave was tinged with sadness. "Some things are easier to repair than others."

Hadrian rose and walked to the cart, snagging a golden chalice. He took a sip of the perfectly warmed blood as he walked to the window. Drawing aside the sheer curtain, he looked downward.

Connie was there, ringing the bell. Soliciting alms from those who passed by.

She looked up at the window.

Had she sensed his presence?

He shifted away, unable to deal with facing her, but encountering George's condemning gaze was no easier.

Pulling back his shoulders, he laid one hand on his hip and said, "What would you have me do? Chase after her when there are hundreds of free meals just walking around the city for my taking?"

George grasped the handle of the cart and flexed his hands. "Is that all she was, sir? A take-out dinner?"

When his keeper said it so casually, anger rose up in him, but not at George. "Leave now."

Hadrian was already striding back to the window when he heard the loud slam of the door behind him.

His keeper was annoyed with him, which was fine.

He was angry at himself for many reasons, most of them revolving around the bell-ringing Santa down below.

When he arrived at the window, he peered down once again, reminding himself that once the Christmas season was gone, she would be also.

It was just as well.

Fate had called once again with another Christmas season filled with pain, only this time, the pain was of his own making.

Who knew breaking a promise could bring such misery?

Briefcase in hand, the man walked past her, but then pivoted abruptly and returned. He looked at her in confusion, as if not sure of why he was there and what he was doing, but then he placed his briefcase down, reached into his suit jacket pocket and removed his wallet.

He rifled through the bills before removing all of them and tossing them into the collection kettle.

Baffled, she said, "Thank you, I think."

With a similarly confused look on his face, he put his wallet back into his suit, grabbed his briefcase and walked away.

She glanced up at the window, wondering. Then she began to ring her bell again, slowly at first but then with more fervor. Wanting to annoy him. Wanting to remind him that she was…

What? Still there? Still within his control if he wanted to reach out and use his power?

A young Goth girl approached, dressed totally in black from head to toe. The metal chains dangling from her jeans jangled almost like small bells in the night. Her pace was sharp and fast as she neared, clearly on her way to something important.

The closer she got, however, the more her gait slowed until the Goth stopped before the kettle, dug into her black leather jacket pocket and extracted a handful of change. She flung it into the kettle, the change merrily clinking against the rim before dropping onto the businessman's pile of bills.

Then the Goth girl hurried away, her pace as determined as it had been before she reached Connie.

Hadrian was behind this.

She hurried across the street, but paused at the stoop. Taking a deep breath, she fortified herself, walked up the steps and briskly knocked on the door.

George answered, a surprised look on his wizened face.

"Tell him to stop. Filling that collection kettle won't make me go away."

A sad smile swept across his keeper's lips. "What makes you think he wants you to go away?"

She shot a glance at the uppermost floor. Watched as the curtain fell back into place. She thought of all the Christmases he had spent in misery. Of the emptiness in his life and possibly in her own.

He had connected with her and she with him, only...

"He broke a promise to me, George."

His keeper bobbed his head in acknowledgement. "He understands that, miss."

She considered George's statement and Hadrian's actions. The promise that he would never leave her be and yet...

"I'm not on Santa duty tomorrow. I'd like to ask a favor of you."

The bob of George's head was coupled with a smile this time. "Ask away, miss."

Connie fidgeted with the silverware on the table one last time before sitting down to await dusk and Hadrian's rising.

She had asked George to make Hadrian's favorite meal and she'd dressed in one of her special holiday outfits—a velvet gown the color of rich burgundy. She had been told the color went well with her olive skin and chestnut-colored hair. Plus, the neckline showed off some of her best attributes while thinning her rather ample hips.

She wanted to please him, although she had struggled with the reasons why for the past day. Everything and anything logical said she should hate him. He had taken her captive. Violated her body by feeding from her. Shattered her trust by breaking his vow.

Yet she was still here, eagerly waiting for him to rise. Possibly in more ways than one.

She was sure others might say it was the Stockholm Syndrome and that she had some kind of twisted connection to her captor. She had certainly considered that probability long and hard during the course of the night and day.

But the reality of it was, she had a good heart and that good heart had seen the sadness in his. She had recognized there was love and compassion buried by the losses he had suffered in his life.

The rustle of the bedcovers pulled her attention from her musings and to Hadrian as he stretched and then sat up in bed, his dark hair tousled from sleep. His body was as magnificent as she remembered, with not a mark on it from the stake she had put to his chest two days before.

He stilled as he saw her sitting there, then he dragged a shaky hand through the longish locks. "I didn't expect you to return."

"I didn't, either."

"Then why are you here?" He reached for something at the foot of the bed—a deep blue robe that he quickly pulled on, hiding his body from her sight. He rose and walked toward her then, tightly belting the robe as he did so.

She stood and motioned to the meal. "Tomorrow is my last day as Santa. After that I'll be gone and I thought…"

What had she thought? she asked herself. Even now she still battled with herself over the reasons she was here. Unable to finish, she jerkily pointed at the small gift sitting on his dinner plate.

"I just wanted to bring you something. To make this Christmas less—"

"Hurtful?" He arched a brow and snagged the small, gaily wrapped box from the plate.

"Fate brought us together for a reason, Hadrian."

He laughed harshly and toyed with the ribbon on the gift. "Fate has delighted in destroying more than one holiday for me, so what will it bring me this year?"

"Hope," she said, finally realizing the reason she had come back. "Hope that this Christmas and the next will bring something different."

He chuckled again, but there was a distinct tone in this laughter. Something lighter, as if he were actually taking her words to heart. "You are an interesting woman, Connie."

She motioned to the gift he still held in his hands. "Open it."

He juggled it back and forth in his hands once again before quickly ripping off the ribbon and wrapping. He hesitated at the lid of the box, shooting her a questioning glance before finally pulling it off.

A bright smile erupted on his face. He shook his head, laughed a little harder and more gleefully as he removed the water ball with the large Santa in the middle of the Christmas scene.

"It plays 'The Twelve Days of Christmas,'" she said as she reached for the water ball, her hands touching his when she gave a twist on the winding mechanism. The music spewed forth, tinkling little bells playing the tune.

"Thank you. It will always remind me of you."

She knew his words were intended to set her free from his earlier threat that he would never let her be. She needed to reciprocate. Twining her fingers through his, she said, "We've yet to start celebrating the twelve days of Christmas."

Hadrian pondered her statement and the gift. Not wanting to assume that either meant more than it did, he said, "Are all lawyers so obtuse—"

"We're trained to be that way."

"I'll take that to mean I may see you again."

She smiled and swung their joined hands

together playfully. "You've still got one more day to make a donation."

With his free hand he pulled out a chair for her at the table. "Doesn't it count that I convinced all those people yesterday—"

"Definitely not. In fact, I feel guilty that I took their money," she said as she sat down and pulled her hand from his so that she might serve him from one of the platters on the table.

"*Cara,* you can't possibly be that honest. You're a lawyer, after all."

She chuckled and spooned some of the soup into his bowl. "Rule two is going to be no more lawyer jokes."

After she had served herself some soup and met his gaze, he asked, "So what's rule one?"

"No biting…unless I ask, of course."

"I'm assuming the same rules apply to me?" He arched a brow and when she turned the full force of her gaze on him, desire flared to life.

"Do you want me to bite?" The quaver in her voice and the tremble in her hand as she brought her spoon to the bowl told him she was not unaffected by the possibility.

Determined to find out if it was good or bad, he said, "Would you bite me now?"

The hand holding the spoon rattled against the edge of the bowl, but then a wicked grin crept across her lips. "Wouldn't you rather save the desserts for last?"

His erection jumped to life as he imagined being dessert for a change. "A wonderful suggestion, *cara*."

He didn't know whether it was their haste to get to the sweets or the absolutely splendid meal and company that made the night pass quickly. The dinner had been composed of many of his favorites, from the soup to the veal marsala with gnocchi in a creamy portobello mushroom sauce. They had shared the meal as lovers might, seated side by side, feeding each other on occasion. Leaning close so that their legs or arms brushed each other when they moved.

Now it was time for the sweets and George had opted for simplicity. Whole succulent ripe strawberries rested on a plate beside a smaller bowl with a balsamic vinegar reduction.

Connie eyed the combo with trepidation, but Hadrian picked up a berry, dipped it in the reduction and brought it to her lips. She took it into her mouth and then, wide-eyed, covered her mouth with her hand as she said, "Oh, my God, that's delicious."

He dipped another berry and popped it into his mouth. The flavors exploded there. The berries were sweet while the balsamic reduction was earthy and slightly tart. He was reaching for another when she stilled his hand and picked up a strawberry. She dipped it and shifted close, her one leg between his thighs, the other on the outside.

She bit into the berry and the juices stained her lips. She was about to lick them away when he said, "Don't."

With his gaze firmly settled on her mouth, he moved the final few inches to bring them close. Cradling the back of her head, he slowly licked the juices from her mouth and then slipped his tongue within.

The berries might have been sweet, but her mouth was even tastier, and the caress of her tongue against his, gentle and seeking, roused him like nothing else. He answered that caress by deepening the kiss, his lips savoring every contour of her mouth and accepting the thrust of her tongue.

When they finally broke apart, they were both breathing heavily and trembling.

As Connie looked at him, she realized that she still held the strawberry. The juice from the berry and the balsamic reduction had left a smear of red-brown in the middle of his chest.

"I guess I should do something about this," she said, tossing the berry onto a plate and grabbing a napkin.

He snagged her hand when it was halfway to his chest. She shot him a quick glance and noted the gleam in his dark eyes.

"Maybe a lick before you bite?"

A frisson of desire raced across her nerve endings, but then she leaned forward and parted the edges of the robe just a bit wider, exposing more of his chest.

His skin had an olive cast, but with a paleness she assumed came from being a vampire. The darker color of his skin matched the deep toffee color of his nipples.

Tentatively she ran the back of her hand across the hair of his chest, before moving it to one nipple, where she passed it back and forth in a lazy motion as she bent close to lick him. With a few slow swipes of her tongue, she removed the juices from his smooth, cool skin, but she didn't stop there.

Moving her head, she slipped her mouth over the beaded tip of his nipple. She kissed the hard nub before running her tongue around the edge of it.

When she sat up, his body was tense. His erection rock hard and thrusting upward beneath the fabric of his velvet robe.

She reached out and wrapped her hand around that erection, stroked him through the soft velvet of the fabric. As she did so, she looked up at him and watched the play of emotions across his face.

Desire was plainly obvious, but behind that lurked other emotions. Gratitude. Happiness. Possibly a hint of admiration.

She wondered about the latter until he said, "You're stronger than most vampires I know."

Connie smiled and chuckled. "I'm Cuban. We can be stubborn."

She was still stroking him and his body jumped a bit as she tightened the caress of her hand.

"*Cara,* you're going to unman me."

A strange choice of words in his case as she remembered how passion had brought forth the demon who hungered for blood and not love.

"I want the man to stay with me, Hadrian. I want it to be the man who shares my body."

Hadrian recalled their passion of two nights ago—freely given and unrestrained. He nearly came then at the thought of her willing and eager beneath him, but he took a shaky breath to quell his desire. When he came, he wanted to be buried deep within her, sharing their mutual passion.

"I want to be a man for you, *cara.*" He raised his hand and laid it in the gap exposed by the neckline of her dress. The rich burgundy made her skin gleam with life. He stroked his fingers along the gap and she said, "I want you to touch me."

He didn't, keeping his hand away from where she wanted it most. "On one condition."

"One?" she whispered and rubbed her lips against his with a breathy sigh.

"Tell me about yourself."

Connie chuckled against his lips. "You're determined, aren't you?"

Hadrian smiled and slowly inched his hand beneath the fabric until he had palmed her breast. Need rippled across her body and with a soft moan she said, "Okay, you win. I'm the middle child."

"That would explain your independent streak," he said. He kissed her while he rubbed his thumb across her taut nipple.

"My older sister thinks I'm obstinate," Connie somehow managed to say as his touch dragged another moan from her. She gazed down, watching the movement of his hand beneath the velvet fabric. Then she moved her own along the cloth covering his erection, dragging a groan from him.

"You're so warm," he said as he slipped her breast free of the dress, but he never stopped touching her.

She did the same, revealing him. Stroking her hand up and down the hard length of him.

"Tell me more," he said and bent his head, licking the tip of her breast.

She cradled his head to her. "I work too much."

"Why?" he murmured before he sucked her hard nipple into his mouth.

"Because until I met you, there was nothing interesting in my life."

He bolted upright and cradled her cheek. "*Cara*, your fascination is—"

"Misplaced? Because I'm—"

"Alive and I can bring you nothing but death," he said sadly and pulled away from her.

"You know that's not true. You've brought me passion—"

"Vampire tricks, *amore*. Nothing more."

He was lying. What they had shared the other night and again today had been real. Not a product of his vampire thrall, but she understood why he was pushing her away—he was still as uncertain as she about their mutual attraction.

Rearranging the front of her dress, she rose and said, "You know where I'll be tomorrow."

"Tormenting me again. Please go," he said as he pulled his robe back on and jerked the belt tight, hiding himself beneath the protection of the fabric.

Gathering herself, she left, realizing as she did so that this might be the last time she saw him.

Pain erupted in the middle of her chest, but she drove it away.

He had given her his Christmas gift—freedom.

She'd be a fool not to accept it.

Chapter 14

"*Sí, mami*. I will definitely be there," she said, confirming to her mother yet again that she could make it to their family gathering on Christmas Eve.

She had done the unthinkable and skipped the last two, choosing to help out fellow colleagues on some cases that had demanded working through the holidays. She might have done the same this year only there hadn't been any matters requiring immediate attention. In fact, it had promised to be such a slow week that she'd taken the week off.

It wasn't that she didn't like her family…she did. And she enjoyed seeing all her little nieces and nephews, only they were sometimes a painful reminder that work alone wasn't enough to fulfill her. Her sisters somehow managed to have both careers and families.

She told herself it was no big deal that at thirty she hadn't found someone to share her life with, but that big biological clock inside of her chimed away its impatient reminder more often than she cared to admit.

Much as she had told Hadrian last night, she had never met anyone as interesting as he was, but she also understood how right he was about what he could offer her.

As she finished her Christmas shopping, preparing for the visit to her family in a few days, she drove him from her mind and told herself that it was better that he not show up tonight at her collection kettle. A clean break would help her forget him, forget the passion that had painfully brought home all that she was missing in her life.

But when she dragged the Santa suit from her closet and began to dress, there was no denying that a part of her wished she would see him.

The water globe sat beside his empty chalice of blood.

Hadrian picked up the globe, shook it, placed it back on the table and watched the swirling bits of fake snow and glitter as they twirled around the Santa.

From outside came the regular chiming of the

bell, calling to him, but he had been ignoring it for most of the night, telling himself that heeding its entreaty would bring them both nothing but pain.

Hadrian knew she wouldn't be out there for much longer. It was nearly nine and the library would soon close. Foot traffic would die down after that, leaving her no reason to stay at her spot.

But nine came and went as did ten and the bell continued to chime until he could no longer avoid its summoning.

He dressed quickly and was on his way down the stairs when the ringing stopped. He paused as well, telling himself that he had lost his chance, until the bell began to ring wildly, all rhythm gone before silence filled the night.

Something was wrong.

He rushed down the stairs and across the street to where Connie lay on the ground, her collection kettle overturned beside her, change littering the ground. The bell silent in her hand.

As he bent and took her into his arms, he smelled the blood. Steam rose from the center of her body into the night air. He ripped open the front of the Santa jacket and her blood warmed the palm of his hand.

She had been knifed. The regular spurt of blood escaping her body told him that her attacker had slashed an artery.

He pressed his hand to the wound and looked

around wildly for help, but the area was devoid of any people since it was late. He summoned George silently and concentrated on what he could do for Connie.

Her face was already growing pale as her life's blood leaked through his fingers. He whispered her name and when she didn't respond, he repeated it, a little more strongly.

She roused, her eyelids fluttering up and down as she struggled for consciousness. She whispered something, only he barely heard her, even with his vampire hearing. He cradled her close and whispered in her ear, "Do not leave me."

This time he did hear her barely audible words.

"Do you believe in Fate, Hadrian?"

He glanced down at her face and then at the blood escaping from her body at an alarming pace. George arrived then, but stopped abruptly, his gaze drifting to the sidewalk beside them.

Hadrian looked there as well and noted the growing pool of blood. He met George's gaze and recognized the sadness there.

As he peered down at Connie once again, he allowed the vampire to emerge and heard the erratic beat of her heart, frantically trying to maintain life. Slowing as life failed.

Her words battered his brain.

Do you believe in Fate, Hadrian?

Fate.

It had brought him nothing but death and here it was again, he thought as he held her close and felt her life fading.

"Hadrian," George said and laid a gentle hand on his shoulder.

He looked to his keeper, who motioned to Connie and said, "It doesn't have to end this way."

Do you believe in Fate, Hadrian? He dared not hope. Dared not believe that this time Fate had a different plan in mind. But even as he struggled to believe, he realized he couldn't hesitate for much longer. Her heart faltered and the time between each beat lengthened. Each beat grew weaker.

Do you believe in Fate? he asked himself, but even as he did so, he returned to his bedroom in a burst of vampire speed and tenderly laid Connie on the bed.

He freed the vampire and bent his head to her neck, felt the last remaining vestiges of life in her body, stubbornly refusing to give up.

Driving his fangs into her neck, he fed from her and bestowed the ultimate kiss. Beneath his fangs came the first stirrings of something different in her body and he picked her up once again.

Her eyelids fluttered open and he slashed his wrist with his fangs and brought the wrist to her mouth, but even as he did so, he said, "If you do not feed now, the transformation will end."

And you will die, he thought, but he didn't say it. He knew she understood, but there was no hesitation as she closed her mouth over his wrist and fed.

His body responded to the pull of her lips against his flesh. To the smell of the blood from both their bodies. As he gazed down at where she had been knifed, there was no fresh blood flowing. The healing powers of the vampire blood now racing through her veins were already at work.

But so was the passion of the vampire's kiss. His body was rock-hard, almost painfully so.

As she finished feeding and sucked in a shaky breath, she moaned and asked, "What is this?"

"The ultimate passion," he answered, bending his head to lick the remnants of his blood from her lips. As he did so, he sensed the heat of her body, beyond that of the human, as the transformation continued.

Connie held on to his shoulders as everything around her and in her shifted with alarming speed. Need grew in her, both for possession and to be possessed, nearly painful in its intensity and she knew he felt it as well. Beneath her hands his body trembled as he restrained himself.

"What do you fear?" she asked.

"If we consummate this passion now…there could be consequences." The strain of emotion, intense, dark and hopeful, filled his voice.

She cradled his face—a face that had grown dear

to her in just a few short days—in her hands and said, "Then let Fate bring you life this Christmas."

He muttered an expletive before he lifted her from the bed and took her to his bathroom, where he gently undressed her, tossing away the blood-stained Santa suit and thermal undergarments.

When she stood before him naked, her body burning up with heat and stained with her blood, he gently took her into his arms and whispered, "You will never regret this choice."

He reached past her to the glass doors of the large shower and opened it. He walked them in and then turned on the water, which sprang at them from all sides, washing away the evidence of the earlier violence. All that remained of her knife wound was a pink line across her midsection.

Steam quickly filled the space of the shower from the warmth of the water, but with the change surging through her, it felt chilled on her skin. As he embraced her, his body was even colder and she shivered.

He laid his forehead against hers. "This is the heat of the vampire. Once the change is complete, you will feel it only when you let the demon take control."

She understood that when the human was in power, the chill of death would mark her skin because she was...

Dead.

Had he not turned her as she had asked, her life

would be over. But it wasn't, and in his arms there was the promise of still more.

"Love me, Hadrian," she said and laid a hand over his heart, which thumped strongly beneath her hand.

Ever thoughtful, he began, "Are you—"

"Sure? More than you can know."

Tension escaped from his body beneath her hand, the way the hesitation washed away with the water streaming down their bodies.

He bent down from his greater height and kissed her, holding her tight against him as he devoured her mouth with his, murmuring soft words of love in a language that needed no translation.

They were both breathing raggedly when he shifted, lowering himself to suckle her breasts and intensify the need building inside of her. She begged him then for fulfillment, needing no further preliminaries, and he complied, easing one thigh between her legs and finding the center of her. Slowly he eased himself within, stretching her and igniting yet more heat as he penetrated her.

She grabbed his shoulders and wrapped her legs around his hips, deepening his possession.

He groaned and splayed one hand across the small of her back, while bracing the other on the wall of the shower stall. He met her gaze as he shifted his hips and drove upward, yanking a startled gasp from her due to the strength of his thrust.

"Did I hurt you, *cara*?" he asked, but didn't wait for her answer to bend his head and tug at her distended nipple with his mouth.

She held his head to her with one hand, using the other to steady her as she moved her hips and rode him, the heat of the water nothing compared to that which was building in their bodies.

The climax that came was swift and punishing, leaving them clinging to one another as if separation would bring pain.

And maybe it would, she thought, holding him tight to her even after he had slipped from her body.

He, too, refused to lose his connection since he somehow managed to grab a towel and wrap them in it, their damp bodies fused together. He returned to life more quickly than she had imagined. When he eased within her again, she was still slick and swollen from their earlier lovemaking. The friction of him moving within quickly pulled a release from her, but he remained rock-hard as he walked her back to the bed and laid her on the edge so he could touch her while he continued his slow, tantalizing strokes.

As he caressed her nipples, rotating them with his fingers, she came again, her body arching off the bed, begging for more, and he gave it, moving one hand down to put pressure on the aching nub of her clitoris. Rubbing it and intensifying the release ripping through her body until he gave one last powerful thrust and came again. His body shuddered from the force of his release.

When he dropped down onto her, he was trembling and she felt the heat of his body.

As he raised himself up on one hand, he wore his demon face and something inside of her responded. Heat erupted inside of her, nearly searing her body from its strength. She knew what he wanted, what was needed to finish this coupling, but he asked anyway.

"Bite me, *cara*. Make me yours," he said and she lifted her head and sank her fangs into his neck.

"Are you sure about this?" he asked even as he ran a possessive hand across her belly.

She rested her hand over his, knowing as he did that new life grew within her. It had only been two days since he had turned her, but she had quickly come to realize in that time just how much a vampire was attuned to not only all around them, but also to the demands and state of their own bodies.

It was how she knew that Fate had brought them both wondrous gifts that Christmas.

A moment later, the door opened and her mother stood there, a bright smile on her face.

"*Mi'ja.* You didn't tell me you were bringing anyone."

Connie smiled and twined her fingers with his.

"Mami, I want you to meet Hadrian."

* * * * *

Turn the page for a sneak preview
of the first book in the new miniseries
DIAMONDS DOWN UNDER
from Silhouette Desire®,
VOWS & A VENGEFUL GROOM
by Bronwyn Jameson

Available January 2008
(SD #1843)

Silhouette Desire®
Always Powerful, Passionate and Provocative

Kimberley Blackstone didn't notice the waiting horde of media until it was too late. Flashbulbs exploded around her like a New Year's light show. She skidded to a halt, so abruptly her trailing suitcase all but overtook her.

This had to be a case of mistaken identity. Surely. Kimberley hadn't been on the paparazzi hit list for close to a decade, not since she'd estranged herself from her billionaire father and his headline-hungry diamond business.

But no, it was *her* name they called. *Her* face was the focus of a swarm of lenses that circled her like avid hornets. Her heart started to pound with fear-fueled adrenaline.

What did they want?

What was going on?

With a rising sense of bewilderment she scanned the crowd for a clue, and her gaze fastened on a tall, leonine figure forcing his way to the front. A tall, familiar figure. Her head came up in stunned recognition, and their gazes collided across the sea of heads before the cameras erupted with another barrage of flashes, this time right in her exposed face.

Blinded by the flashbulbs—and by the shock of that momentary eye-meet—Kimberley didn't realize his intent until he'd forged his way to her side, possibly by the sheer strength of his personality. She felt his arm wrap around her shoulder, pulling her into the protective shelter of his body, allowing her no time to object. No chance to lift her hands to ward him off.

In the space of a hastily drawn breath, she found herself plastered knee-to-nose against six feet two inches of hard-bodied male.

Ric Perrini.

Her lover for ten torrid weeks, her husband for ten tumultuous days.

Her ex for ten tranquil years.

After all this time, he should not have felt so familiar but, oh dear, he did. She knew the scent of that body and its lean, muscular strength. She knew its heat and its slick power and every response it could draw from hers.

She also recognized the ease with which he'd taken control of the moment and the decisiveness of his deep voice when it rumbled close to her ear. "I have a car waiting outside. Is this your only luggage?"

Kimberley nodded. "I assume you will tell me," she said tightly, "what this welcome party is all about."

"Not while the welcome party is within earshot. No."

Barking a request for the cameramen to stand aside, Perrini took her hand and pulled her into step with his ground-eating stride. Kimberley let him, because he was right, damn his arrogant, Italian-suited hide. Despite the speed with which he whisked her across the airport terminal, she could almost feel the hot breath of the pursuing media on her back.

This was neither the time nor the place for explanations. Inside his car, however, she would get answers.

Now that the initial shock had been blown away—by the haste of their retreat, by the heat of her gathering indignation, by the rush of adrenaline fired by Perrini's presence and the looming verbal battle—her brain was starting to tick over. This had to be her father's doing. And if it was a Howard Blackstone publicity ploy, then it had to be about Blackstone Diamonds, the company that ruled his life.

The knowledge made her chest tighten with a familiar ache of disillusionment.

She'd known her father would be flying in from Sydney for today's opening of the newest in his chain of exclusive, high-end jewelry boutiques. The opulent shopfront sat adjacent to the rival business where Kimberley worked. No coincidence, she thought bitterly, just as it was no coincidence that Ric Perrini was here in Auckland ushering her to his car.

Perrini was Howard Blackstone's right-hand man, second in command at Blackstone Diamonds, a legacy of his short-lived marriage to the boss's daughter. No doubt her father had sent him to fetch her; the question was *why?*

* * * * *

Get swept away down under with the glitz and glamour of the Blackstone empire as Kimberley tries to determine the real reason behind her "reunion" with Ric....

Look for VOWS & A VENGEFUL GROOM
by Bronwyn Jameson,
in stores January 2008.

To fulfill his father's dying wish,
Greek tycoon Christos Niarchos must
marry Ava Monroe, a woman who
betrayed him years ago. But his soon-to-
be-wife has a secret that could rock
more than his passion for her.

Look for

THE GREEK
TYCOON'S
SECRET HEIR

by

KATHERINE
GARBERA

Available January wherever you buy books

Visit Silhouette Books at www.eHarlequin.com   SD76845

REQUEST YOUR FREE BOOKS!

2 FREE NOVELS PLUS 2 FREE GIFTS!

Silhouette®

nocturne™

Dramatic and Sensual Tales of Paranormal Romance.

YES! Please send me 2 FREE Silhouette® Nocturne™ novels and my 2 FREE gifts. After receiving them, if I don't wish to receive any more books, I can return the shipping statement marked "cancel." If I don't cancel, I will receive 4 brand-new novels every other month and be billed just $4.47 per book in the U.S. or $4.99 per book in Canada, plus 25¢ shipping and handling per book plus applicable taxes, if any*. That's a savings of about 15% off the cover price! I understand that accepting the 2 free books and gifts places me under no obligation to buy anything. I can always return a shipment and cancel at any time. Even if I never buy another book from Silhouette, the two free books and gifts are mine to keep forever.

238 SDN ELS4 338 SDN ELXG

Name _____ (PLEASE PRINT) _____

Address _____ Apt. # _____

City _____ State/Prov. _____ Zip/Postal Code _____

Signature (if under 18, a parent or guardian must sign)

Mail to the Silhouette Reader Service™:
IN U.S.A.: P.O. Box 1867, Buffalo, NY 14240-1867
IN CANADA: P.O. Box 609, Fort Erie, Ontario L2A 5X3

Not valid to current Silhouette Nocturne subscribers.

Want to try two free books from another line?
Call 1-800-873-8635 or visit www.morefreebooks.com.

* Terms and prices subject to change without notice. NY residents add applicable sales tax. Canadian residents will be charged applicable provincial taxes and GST. This offer is limited to one order per household. All orders subject to approval. Credit or debit balances in a customer's account(s) may be offset by any other outstanding balance owed by or to the customer. Please allow 4 to 6 weeks for delivery.

Your Privacy: Silhouette is committed to protecting your privacy. Our Privacy Policy is available online at www.eHarlequin.com or upon request from the Reader Service. From time to time we make our lists of customers available to reputable firms who may have a product or service of interest to you. If you would prefer we not share your name and address, please check here. ☐

SN07

Inside ROMANCE

Stay up-to-date on all your romance reading news!

Inside Romance is a FREE quarterly newsletter highlighting our upcoming series releases and promotions.

Visit

www.eHarlequin.com/InsideRomance

to sign up to receive our complimentary newsletter today!

IRN11 07

New York Times
bestselling author

MAGGIE SHAYNE

Even by vampire standards Reaper
is a loner, and his current mission to
destroy a gang of rogue bloodsuckers
is definitely a one-vamp job. Then fate
takes a hand, and before he knows it,
he's surrounded by a ragtag crew of
misfit helpers.

Seth is new to immortality, but he's
sharp and strong—and he'll risk
anything for the rogues' strange
female captive, Vixen.

Vixen is confused by the emotions
that swirl through her at the sight of
her impulsive hero. She only hopes
the brutal Gregor and his bloodthirsty
renegades will leave her alive long
enough to explore them.

Or will Reaper himself be the one to
destroy them all?

DEMON'S KISS

"Maggie Shayne has a talent for
taking characters born in fantasy
and making them come alive."
—*Romantic Times BOOKreviews*

*Available the first week of December
2007 wherever paperbacks are sold!*
www.MIRABooks.com

MIRA®

MMS2497

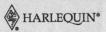 HARLEQUIN®

INTRIGUE®

INTRIGUE'S ULTIMATE HEROES

6 heroes. 6 stories.
One month to read them all.

For one special month, Harlequin Intrigue
is dedicated to those heroes among men.
Desirable doctors, sexy soldiers, brave
bodyguards—they are all
Intrigue's Ultimate Heroes.

In January, collect all 6.

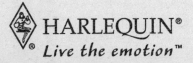 HARLEQUIN®
Live the emotion™

www.eHarlequin.com   HI69302

Silhouette

nocturne™

COMING NEXT MONTH

#31 SCIONS: RESURRECTION • Patrice Michelle

Scions (Book 1 of 3)

A rebel amongst vampires, Jachin Black was forced to
live among humans. Until Ariel Swanson became the
most dangerous—and desired—human. With her in
his possession, Jachin could reclaim leadership over his
people. But dare he believe their union could also fulfill
an age-old prophecy uniting two sworn enemies?

#32 GUARDIAN'S KEEP • Lori Devoti

When Kelly Shane challenged Kol Hildr for control over
his portal to the paranormal realm, the battle between
witch and shape-shifter threatened even the gods. But
would Kol be able to show Kelly why only the strongest
became guardians, before Kelly was seduced by darker
powers? And before Kol had to make a choice between
duty and desire…?